"What a funny fireman!" cried Freddie.

The Bobbsey Twins at Spruce Lake

The Bobbsey Twins at Spruce Lake

BY
LAURA LEE HOPE

AUTHOR OF "THE BOBBSEY TWINS SERIES," "THE
BUNNY BROWN SERIES," "THE SIX LITTLE
BUNKERS SERIES," "THE OUTDOOR GIRLS
SERIES," ETC.

NEW YORK
GROSSET & DUNLAP
PUBLISHERS

Made in the United States of America

CONTENTS

THE BOBBSEY TWINS
AT SPRUCE LAKE

CHAPTER I

A SUDDEN SHOWER

"SAY, Flossie!"

"What you want, Freddie?"

Two little children were playing on the shady front porch of their home. They were twins—you could tell that just by one look at them for they looked much alike with their blue eyes and light, fluffy hair. Only, of course, Freddie wouldn't want you to think he was a girl any more than his sister Flossie would want you to think she was a boy.

"When are you going to take your dolls off this porch?" Freddie asked his sister. "Come on. I'm in a hurry."

"I'm not going to take my dolls off this

porch, Freddie Bobbsey, so there!" exclaimed Flossie. "I don't care if you are in a hurry," and she finished buttoning the dress of a new doll named Goldie. "I'm going to stay right here."

"You can't!" said Freddie, and he shook his head earnestly. "You've got to get off! But I'll wait a little while—until you finish dressing your doll."

Freddie walked toward the other side of the porch and Flossie soon heard the rumble of iron wheels over the boards.

"Why have I got to get off here?" asked the little girl, shaking her head in order to toss her golden curls out of her eyes. "I want to stay here and make a party for my dolls."

"Nope!" Freddie shook his head hard. "You can't," he went on.

"Why not?"

Flossie was just as "set" in her way as her brother was in his.

"I have to wash this porch with my new fire engine, and if you stay here you'll get all wet," Freddie answered.

"I don't care." Flossie went on smoothing out the dress of her newest doll. "Go on and wet me if you want to. It's a nice warm day and I have on old things. Squirt your fire engine all you want to."

This did not suit Freddie. He wanted the porch clear for his hose work. So he spoke to his sister again.

"Maybe you don't care if you get wet," he said; "but your dolls will get all wet, too."

"Don't you dare, Freddie Bobbsey!" cried Flossie. "If you squirt any water on even my oldest rag doll I'll tell Mother!"

"Then you'd better get off this porch," went on the blue-eyed boy. "I won't wet you or your dolls on purpose, but my new fire engine squirts hard and if you get sprinkled it won't be my fault and I'll tell Mother so." Again Flossie heard the rumble of iron wheels coming nearer her corner of the porch.

She knew that rumble well. Freddie, who, ever since he was very, very little, had been much interested in fires and fire engines, was now pulling across the porch his very latest toy of this sort. It was a large fire engine—that is, large for a toy—and it had a real rubber hose on it, a pump worked by a spring, and a tank of water.

When the tank of water was filled and the spring pump started, a stream of water would spurt out of the hose and spray perhaps ten feet in the air. Freddie was very proud of his new toy.

Of course he was never allowed to make a real fire on which to try his engine. Mrs. Bobbsey was always very careful about this and Freddie minded. Once, when he was a very little boy, he got hold of some matches and lighted them to make a fire. But his fingers were burned, and that taught Freddie such a good lesson that, never since, had he played with fire.

But he had lots of fun with one toy fire engine after another, and put out any number of "make-believe" fires. Sometimes Flossie would pretend that her dolls' house was burning and Freddie would dash up with his toy engine and squirt real water.

He was anxious now to try what the hose of his fire engine would do toward washing down the front porch. But he knew he could not make what Sam Johnson would call "a good job of it" unless Flossie and her dolls were out of the way. So Freddie pulled his rumbling,

iron fire engine close to where his sister was
sitting with her half dozen dolls and said:

"Look! The tank's full."

"I don't care," said Flossie, not turning her
head but taking up another doll to make a
change in her dress.

"And I have the pump all wound up," went
on Freddie.

"I don't care."

"And my hose is all ready to squirt."

"Pooh! Think I care?" murmured Flossie,
holding her doll off at arm's length to see how
the changed dress looked.

"Aw, say!" and Freddie's voice was teasing
now, "please get off the porch so I can wash
it nice and clean. You can come back after I
get through."

"No," said Flossie, shaking her head hard.
"It will be all wet if you squirt water on this
porch and then I can't sit here with my dolls.
You wait until I get through and then you can
squirt."

Freddie thought about this for a moment,
but he was never very patient. If he wanted to
do a thing he wanted to do it. He didn't like to
wait. He was all ready to start his engine and

he was anxious to hear the whir of the pump
and the splash of the water from the little
hose.

But Flossie was just as firm in making up
her mind to stay where she was. Freddie
thought for a moment and then said:

"Didn't we have fun at Wide Gate Farm?"

"Yes, we did," agreed Flossie, as she remembered where they had lately spent many happy
vacation weeks. But she did not move.

"Maybe," said Freddie, edging a little closer
with his fire engine, "we'll go up there again
and have more fun. And find more treasure,"
he added.

"No," said Flossie slowly as she opened a
box to take out a hair ribbon for another doll,
"I don't think we shall."

"Why not?" asked Freddie. He thought perhaps if he could get Flossie to talking enough
about Wide Gate Farm she might forget about
staying on the porch and then she would go
off and he could wash it. "Why shouldn't we
go back there?" he asked.

"'Cause," said Flossie, "I heard Mother
and Daddy talking about going to another
place, maybe."

"You did?" cried Freddie, so excited that he dropped the cord by which he had been pulling his engine along. "Where?"

"I heard Mother and Daddy talking about a place called Spruce Lake," said Flossie.

"Where's Spruce Lake?" the golden-haired boy asked.

Flossie shook her head as she put back one ribbon and took out another.

"I don't zackly know," she said. "But it's somewhere."

"Course it's somewhere," agreed Freddie. "But, aw, say, Flossie, get off the porch, will you, so I can hose it? Then we'll go ask Mother where Spruce Lake is and maybe Dinah will give us some cookies and I'll help you carry your dolls off so they won't get wet."

"My dolls aren't going to get wet," said Flossie calmly.

"They'll get wet if you stay here when I start my fire engine and the hose squirts," declared her brother.

"Don't you dare wet me or my dolls!" warned Flossie. "If you do I'll go right in and tell Mother and you know what happened once before when you squirted on me."

"Nothing happened," Freddie said. Sometimes his memory was very short.

"Yes, there did, too!" declared Flossie. "Last time you squirted on me Daddy took the fire engine away from you and he didn't let you have it again for a week."

"Oh—well——" Freddie did not know what to say to this. He made one last appeal. "Please get off the porch, Flossie, so I can squirt!" he begged. "Then you can come back."

"No. I'm not going until I get good and ready."

Flossie could be very stubborn at times.

Freddie's blue eyes snapped. He had a temper of his own at times, though usually he and Flossie played together very well and with few quarrels.

"Wish Bert was here, and Nan," murmured Freddie, as he picked up the cord that hauled his fire engine. "They'd make Flossie move so I could hose the porch."

Bert and Nan were the older Bobbsey twins. They were not at home just now, having gone downtown on an errand for their mother. Freddie hoped they would come back soon.

Several minutes passed and Flossie made no move to get off the porch, a large part of this time she was using to lay out her dolls with their boxes of clothes. So Freddie made up his mind that he must do something. There was a little leak in the tank of his fire engine and the water was slowly dripping out. If he waited too long there would be none left to squirt through the hose.

"Stay there if you want to, then!" Freddie suddenly cried. "I'm going to squirt and if you get wet it won't be my fault."

He dragged his engine farther along and reached to touch the handle that started the spring motor.

"Don't you dare squirt when I'm here!" shouted Flossie. "I was here first and you've got to wait until I go away."

"I'm not going to wait," replied Freddie. "Here she goes!"

There was a whir of the spring and the wheels of the little pump on the fire engine began to turn. Out of the nozzle of the rubber hose sprayed a thin stream of water.

To give Freddie credit, he first aimed the hose at the far end of the porch and away from

Flossie. He thought no water would get on her, at least for a time. He thought his sister would move when he was ready to wash the other end of the porch.

But Freddie did not count on the wind, which was blowing rather hard. It blew the water spray from the hose over on Flossie and she began to get wet.

She jumped to her feet, put aside the doll she had taken up to dress, and, running toward Freddie, cried:

"Stop it! You're wetting me! I'm going to tell Mother! Take your old fire engine away!"

"'Tisn't an old engine—it's new," said Freddie, as he aimed the stream of water along the boards of the porch floor, washing away some specks of dirt.

"Then take your new engine away!" cried Flossie. "Oh, I'm getting all wet!" she screamed, as the wind blew more water on her

"Get off the porch then!" yelled Freddie.

"No!" shouted Flossie.

Just then Bert and Nan, carrying between them a large package, turned in from the side walk. They heard the excited shouts.

"What's the matter, I wonder!" exclaimed Bert.

"Oh, Flossie and Freddie are having a fuss," said Nan. "Oh, look!" she cried. "Freddie is squirting with his fire engine and he's wetting Flossie. Stop it, Freddie! Stop it!" Nan ordered.

She ran forward to make Freddie obey, hurrying up the steps and dragging Bert after her, as he had hold of the package with her. Then, whether he intended to or not it is hard to say, but Freddie aimed the hose straight at Bert and Nan and they got a sudden shower of water, for now the pump on the fire engine was working at full speed.

"Now look what you did!" cried Flossie, dancing about safely out of reach of the spray. "Oh, Freddie Bobbsey!"

"Drop that hose!" ordered Bert.

He spoke so sternly that Freddie obeyed. But the pump kept on working and as the end of the hose was dropped it was aimed at Bert. In an instant he got a good dousing.

"Wow!" he yelled.

"Oh! Oh!" gasped Freddie. Things were getting worse. He hadn't meant to do all this.

More and more water sprayed over Bert and Nan. Flossie was safely out of reach in a corner, dancing up and down and shouting:

"Now you'll get it! You'll get it now, Freddie Bobbsey!"

"Shut that water off!" ordered Bert.

Then he dropped his end of the package he had been carrying with Nan. It fell to the porch floor with a bang and burst open while over it, and over the two older twins, more water sprayed and spurted.

"This is terrible!" cried Nan.

Bert looked at the broken package and said to his brother:

"Now you have done it! Oh, boy!"

He pointed to the broken bundle he and Nan had been carrying. Freddie wondered what was in it. So did Flossie.

CHAPTER II

COOKIES, COOKIES EVERYWHERE

"Turn off that water, Freddie!" cried Bert Bobbsey. "If you don't I'll—plug, blub, I'll, wug——"

He couldn't say any more, for when he tried to talk the water from Freddie's fire engine spurted right into Bert's open mouth, making him choke and gasp.

"I—I can't turn it off!" cried Freddie, for he was out of reach of the toy pump he had started.

"Then I will," declared Bert.

He made a dash toward the engine, which was still spurting water out through the hose. But Bert stepped in a puddle and fell down. At the same time he was reaching out to take hold of Freddie to thrust him aside to reach the engine, and Freddie also fell down.

13

"Oh, what fun!" screamed Flossie, laughing harder than ever.

"Don't laugh!" warned Nan.

"I can't help it," said Flossie. "Look at Bert and Freddie!"

The two boys were wiggling around on the wet porch. Bert's foot suddenly touched the loose hose of the pumping fire engine and aimed it toward Nan. Then she got another shower bath.

Some of the water sprayed on the broken package and, seeing this, Nan made a dash toward it, shouting:

"They'll get all wet and will spoil."

"What will?" asked Flossie, still wondering what was in the bundle Bert and Nan had carried up on the porch.

Before Nan could answer Mrs. Bobbsey and her husband came walking along the street. Mrs. Bobbsey had gone to her husband's office to walk home with him and talk over certain matters.

Mrs. Bobbsey saw the commotion on the porch. She grasped her husband's arm and said:

"Look. Something has happened."

"It seems so," agreed Mr. Bobbsey, for he had a glimpse of Bert and Freddie rolling around, of Flossie laughing and shouting, and of Nan trying to drag the bundle out of reach of the spraying hose.

"Come on!" exclaimed Mrs. Bobbsey, and she and her husband began to run.

"Thank goodness!" murmured Nan, when she saw her father and mother coming. "Things will be all right now."

While the father and mother are on their way to straighten out the tangle of children, a fire engine and a mysterious bundle, just a moment will be taken to tell new readers who the Bobbseys are.

The first book of this series, called "The Bobbsey Twins," tells you that Mr. and Mrs. Richard Bobbsey lived in the Eastern city of Lakeport on Lake Metoka, where Mr. Bobbsey owned a large lumberyard.

The children's names you already know. Flossie and Freddie were the younger twins, and strangers often found it hard to believe that they were brother and sister to Nan and Bert, the older pair of twins, for Flossie and

Freddie had blue eyes and golden hair, while Nan and Bert were dark.

"I suppose Freddie and Flossie will have brown hair when they grow older," Mrs. Bobbsey was used to say, "but I hope they will stay blond for a long time."

Besides the Bobbseys there were two other persons who might be said to be members of the family. These were Sam Johnson and his wife, fat Dinah, the colored cook. Sam did all sorts of work about the Bobbsey home. There was also a dog named Snap and a cat named Snoop. When these animals were younger they were much with the children. But of late years Snap was not so lively and playful, and often Snoop would wander off and be gone for a week at a time.

However, the children did not mind this for they had plenty of fun going to the country, to the seashore, or the mountains with their parents when there was no school.

Their last vacation had been spent at Wide Gate Farm, owned by Mr. Ralston, whom the children called "Grandpa." The jolly fun the twins had there is told about in the book just before this one you are now reading. The book is named "The Bobbsey Twins Treasure Hunting," and you can find out in it just what happened.

There was an old lady named Sallie Pry, who was called "aunt" by the Bobbsey children, though she really was no relation to them. Once Aunt Sallie Pry, who was very deaf, helped Nan and Bert keep house while Mr. and Mrs. Bobbsey were away.

Aunt Sallie Pry was very poor, but she could get some money if a certain piece of land, near Wide Gate Farm, could be sold, for her husband's grandfather had once owned that land.

How the Bobbsey twins found the "treasure" which helped Aunt Sallie get her share of the farm is set down in the book just before this one.

Bert and Nan, with their small brother and sister, had not long been home from Wide Gate Farm when this hose-sprinkling trouble with Freddie's engine started. A queer part of it was that Aunt Sallie Pry had given Freddie money with which to buy the big toy fire engine.

As has been told you, Freddie was "crazy"

about firemen and engines. In fact, his father used to call him his "little fireman," as he used to call Flossie his "fat fairy." Freddie had lots of fun with his new engine, but just now, you may be sure, Bert and Nan wished it did not spray such a powerful stream of water.

"Children! Children!" cried Mrs. Bobbsey, hurrying up on the porch. "What in the world are you doing? Get up, Bert! Don't roll Freddie around that way in the water."

"I'm not rolling him, Mother. He's rolling himself," said Bert, which was true enough.

"Look at the water squirt!" cried Flossie, who, up to this time, had managed to keep out of reach of the hose. But now, all of a sudden, it twisted around and gave her a shower bath. "Oh, Freddie Bobbsey!" she yelled. "Look what you've done with your old engine!"

"Why didn't you get off the porch with your dolls when I had to wash it?" cried Freddie, as he managed to get to his feet while Bert did the same.

"Oh, so you call this washing the porch, do you?" chuckled Mr. Bobbsey, as he stepped over and shut off the spring motor of the toy engine. "Well, it will need it again, I think."

"Oh, such a mess!" sighed Mrs. Bobbsey. "Freddie, you're soaked. And you're wet, too, Bert."

"So am I!" laughed Flossie, and she didn't seem to mind.

"I hope your dress doesn't spot, Nan," went on her mother.

"No'm, I don't think it will," said Nan. "But, Mother, look!"

Nan pointed to the broken package she and Bert had carried up the porch steps. Bert tried to lift one end, and as he did so some smaller packages that were wrapped up in the larger one tumbled out and some brown sugar cookies were scattered over the wet porch floor.

"Oh, look!" cried Flossie, making a dive for some of the cakes.

"Cookies! Cookies! What a lot of cookies!" shouted Freddie.

"Children! Children!" commanded Mrs. Bobbsey. "Stop! You'll drive me crazy! Don't touch those cookies! They're for the church supper, and if they are all wet and spoiled—— Oh, dear!" She seemed much worried.

So that was what the bundle contained—cookies. Flossie and Freddie had been wondering what the secret was. Now it was out. But things seemed to have been spoiled by Freddie's fire engine, for some of the cookies were soaking wet.

"Oh, if they are all spoiled!" murmured Mrs. Bobbsey sadly.

"But they aren't, Mother! See?" exclaimed Nan quickly. "Only a few packages broke open and got wet. All the others are wrapped in waxed paper and water won't hurt them."

"It's lucky Mrs. Porter did that," said Bert, as he began picking up off the wet porch the unopened packages of cakes which, as Nan had said, were wrapped, a dozen each, in rolls of waxed paper that had kept out the water very well.

"Things aren't as bad as they seemed at first," said Mrs. Bobbsey with a sigh of relief as she sat down in a chair which, luckily, had not been wet by Freddie's spurting hose. "Now how did this all happen?" she asked.

"I wanted to wash the porch, but Flossie wouldn't take her dolls off," explained Freddie.

"So he just started up his fire engine when I was here and he got some of my dolls wet and I got wet a little," added Flossie. "Then I was going to make him stop and he dropped the hose and that's how it happened."

"Why didn't you try to stop them?" asked Mrs. Bobbsey, looking first at Nan and then at Bert.

"We weren't here," Nan replied. "We came along just before you got here, Mother."

"We went down to Mrs. Porter's to get the cookies, as you told us," said Bert. Mrs. Bobbsey and Mrs. Porter were arranging a church supper and Mrs. Porter had agreed to bake the cookies—many dozens of them. They were to be taken to the church in the Bobbsey automobile and Nan and Bert had gone after the bundle.

"And it sure is lucky that Mrs. Porter thought to wrap them in waxed paper," said Bert again. "I guess not more than two dozen broke out. Yes, only two packages broke," he went on, as he looked over the large bundle.

"Well, I'm glad of that," his mother said.

"Can we have some of the cookies on the

porch?" asked Freddie, pointing to some that had rolled into corners and so were out of the spraying water from his toy engine.

"Oh, yes, I guess so," said his father. "Pick them up and then go and tell Sam to bring the garden hose and wash down this porch."

"Oh, let me do it with my engine!" cried Freddie.

"No," said his father. "You have done mischief enough in one day with that fire engine of yours, Freddie. Let Sam clean the porch."

"Well, then we'll have a party with the cookies that aren't wet. Come on, Flossie," begged Freddie.

"You mustn't eat those cookies on the porch," said Mrs. Bobbsey. "They'll be dirty."

"I'll wipe 'em clean," offered Freddie, rubbing a sugar cake up and down on the sleeve of his blouse. "The real dirty ones you can give to your dolls, Flossie."

"As if I'd do that!" snapped Flossie. "Go on! I'm not going to play party with you. I'm going to pack my dolls to get ready to go to Spruce Lake."

"Spruce Lake!" exclaimed Bert, who had

come back after carrying the dry cookies into the house. "What about Spruce Lake?"

"Daddy and Mother are going there," said Flossie, beginning to gather up her dolls.

"You are?" gasped Nan. "When? Oh, are we all going?" Her brown eyes were dancing with delight.

"I'm going to take my fire engine to Spruce Lake," announced Freddie.

"Are we going on another vacation?" asked Bert. "Do you think we can find some more treasure, Dad? Oh, what fun!"

"Hurray! Hurray! Hurray!" shouted Flossie and Freddie.

"Spruce Lake was supposed to be a secret," said Mrs. Bobbsey. "I didn't know we'd mentioned it before Flossie and Freddie."

"Oh, Mother! No fair not telling us!" ejaculated Nan. "Go on now, please," she pleaded. "The secret is partly out so you might as well tell it all. Do, Mother!"

"Tell us! Tell us! Let's go to Spruce Lake!" sang Flossie and Freddie. They seemed to have forgotten all about their recent quarrel.

"Oh, my dears, please be quiet!" begged Mrs. Bobbsey.

"I guess the only way we can keep them quiet is to take them to Spruce Lake," chuckled Mr. Bobbsey.

"Oh, Dad, will you?" begged Bert.

"I'll see," said Mr. Bobbsey. "There is still enough of summer left for a vacation in the woods, but I don't know about keeping you children out of school. It's supposed to start soon."

Nan and Bert looked sober, but Flossie and Freddie were still marching about the porch singing:

"We're going to Spruce Lake! We're going to Spruce Lake!"

"Maybe," said Mr. Bobbsey, with a smile. "Now, if you will quiet down, I'll tell you——"

"Hark!" suddenly exclaimed Mrs. Bobbsey, holding up her hand for silence. At that moment fat, black Dinah appeared in the front door and called:

"Tellyfoam, Mr. Bobbsey. Tellyfoam! Dat bell done ring like it was a fire. Somebody want yo' on de tellyfoam."

CHAPTER III

JAKE DOXEY'S STORY

"Wait until I come back from answering the telephone and I will tell you more about Spruce Lake," said Mr. Bobbsey to the children, now seated on a dry part of the porch near their mother in the rocking chair.

"Oh, what fun we'll have!" murmured Flossie.

"'Tisn't sure we're going yet," Nan reminded her.

"Oh, I guess we'll go," declared Freddie. "I'm going to dry out my fire engine and pack it up."

"I'll pack my dolls," said Flossie.

"Gracious, you aren't going to take *all* of them, are you?" asked Nan, with a laugh.

"Well, I'll take my newest, best doll named Goldie," said Flossie.

Then Mr. Bobbsey came back from the

"tellyfoam," as Dinah called it, and said to his wife:

"It's no use. They can't find him. He's lost."

"Who's lost?" asked Bert quickly, remembering a time he himself had once been in that condition.

"Jake Doxey is lost," said Mr. Bobbsey. "They can't find him, and I'm afraid it's going to make trouble."

"Is his mother worried about him?" asked Flossie, and then Mr. Bobbsey laughed. Flossie looked at him queerly.

"Jake Doxey is a big man," said Mrs. Bobbsey, "so I think his mother would not worry much about him, even if she knew he was lost."

"How can a big man get lost?" asked Freddie.

"I see I shall have to tell you the story of Jake Doxey," said Mr. Bobbsey. "And as this porch looks terrible, let's go around to the back yard and sit under the grape arbor while Sam gets out his big hose and washes the place down properly."

"Couldn't I help him?" asked Freddie, who had picked up his toy fire engine, though it was a rather heavy load for him.

"No, indeed!" said Mrs. Bobbsey. "You have played in the water enough to-day. And you'll have to go in and get on dry clothes—all of you!" she said.

"Oh, we're not very wet," said Nan. "It's so warm we're almost dry already. The cookies got the worst of it."

"Not many of them were spoiled," stated Bert, who had carried the broken bundle into the house. "So let's go out in the back yard and hear about lost Jake Doxey. Where is he lost, Dad?"

"Somewhere up around Spruce Lake. That was a telephone message from a man I had hunting for him the past week, saying he had to give up as he couldn't find a trace of Jake."

"Well, come around now and listen to the story," urged Mrs. Bobbsey, making sure that the pieces of cookies that Freddie and Flossie were nibbling on were clean.

"I love to hear Daddy tell stories," murmured Flossie, as she managed to squeeze in beside her father who sat in a rustic garden chair beneath the shady grapevine.

"This isn't a regular story, like the kind that

begins 'once upon a time,' my dear," warned Mr. Bobbsey. "Its just about a missing man."

"What did he miss?" asked Freddie. "The train?"

"He missed seeing me," said Mr. Bobbsey, "and if I can't find him it will mean that we both lose money."

"Oh, it's going to be another treasure hunt, like finding the papers which gave Aunt Sallie Pry her share in the Lapham farm!" exclaimed Nan, her eyes shining. "Isn't it, Daddy?"

"Well, in a way it's a sort of hunt," agreed Mr. Bobbsey. "Only what is missing now is this man Jake Doxey. It's queer where he has gone. Now listen and I'll tell you about him."

Then Mr. Bobbsey related that some years before he had wanted to buy some lumber land up near Spruce Lake, in that part of our country called New England.

"I wanted to get hold of this lumber tract as it had many valuable trees on it," said Mr. Bobbsey, in telling the story.

"What's a lumber tack?" asked Flossie.

"Not *tack*, my dear," explained Nan. "It's *tract*—that means a big piece of country, sometimes meadow and sometimes woods."

"We went to Meadow Brook once and we had lots of fun," said Freddie in a sing-song voice.

"Hush, dear, listen to Dad's story," begged Nan.

"Well, really, it isn't much of a story," said Mr. Bobbsey. "I wanted to buy this tract of valuable timber, or woods, of Jake Doxey, but he and I could not agree on a price. I thought he wanted too much money.

"But I find now I need the land so I can cut down the trees to make lumber and I'll be glad to give Jake what he asked years ago, and even more. But the trouble is I can't find Jake. I've written letters to him, up near Spruce Lake where he used to live, but they all come back from the post office. The postmaster says Jake hasn't called for his mail for a long time.

"A few weeks ago I sent a man up to Spruce Lake to see if he could find Jake, so I could give him money and take his timber tract, but the man came back and said he couldn't find Jake. Then I got some other men, living around Spruce Lake, to try to find Jake, and the one who telephoned to me just now says

Jake seems to have disappeared. So that's all to the story."

" 'Tisn't much of a story," said Flossie, with a little sniff. "Didn't they live happy ever after?"

"Who?" asked Nan, with a laugh.

"Jake Doxey and his wife."

"I don't know that he has a wife," chuckled Mr. Bobbsey. "And I quite agree with you, Flossie, that it isn't much of a story. But I told you, at first, it wouldn't be."

"That's right, you did," stated Freddie, carefully drying his beloved fire engine.

"And what happened next?" asked Nan. She was always a great one for asking this question whenever her father told a story.

"Well, the next thing to do, I suppose," answered Mr. Bobbsey, "is for me to go to Spruce Lake myself and see if I can find Jake Doxey. I am in great need of his land and I can't begin to cut down the trees on it until I pay him the money for it. So I guess I'll have to hunt for Jake myself."

"Will you take us with you?" put in Freddie eagerly.

"What do you know about hunting for lost

men?" asked Bert, with a laugh at his little brother. "You're just a fireman."

"Well, I could catch fish in Spruce Lake," declared Freddie. "When you go to the woods you have to camp out and eat, and fish are good to eat."

"Indeed they are, little fireman!" said his father.

"Oh, are you really going to take us?" asked Nan. "It will be such fun!"

"As if you hadn't had a good summer vacation already!" said her mother. "What about school?"

"Yes, I s'pose we'll have to go back to school soon," sighed Bert. "Oh, dear!"

You might think, from this, that Bert really didn't like school. But you would be wrong to think that, for he was fond of his teachers and his studies. It was just the thought of starting again after the jolly summer vacation that seemed a bit sad.

"I don't see how we can take the children to Spruce Lake with us," said Mrs. Bobbsey, looking at her husband from beneath the shade of the big grapevine. "I don't want them to lose their places in their classes."

"We don't want to stay here if you go off to the woods," said Bert in gloomy tones. "It wouldn't be any fun at all."

"Not even if Aunt Sallie Pry came to help you keep house?" asked his mother, with a smile.

"Oh, Mother! We had a terrible time!" sighed Nan. "Aunt Sallie is as good as she can be, but she is so deaf and her lumbago can't be any better. And now that she has her little treasure, I don't believe she would come and stay with us."

"No, Nan, I don't believe she would," agreed Mrs. Bobbsey, with a laugh. "I was only saying that to tease you."

"Aunt Sallie's terribly deaf," said Freddie. "One day I asked her if I could take the *rake*, and she said she would give me a piece of cake."

"Poor Aunt Sallie Pry!" murmured Mrs. Bobbsey. "She is much happier than she was, now that she has the money which you children helped find for her by the treasure hunt. But what about this Spruce Lake?" she asked Mr. Bobbsey. "Are you really going?"

"Yes, I must go," he answered. "And I'd like to take you with me, my dear."

"What about the children and school?" asked Mrs. Bobbsey.

"I think we can fix that," was her husband's reply. "I heard this noon that because of some repairs that are needed to the school the building may not open until late in October, instead of early in September. So we might all manage to go to Spruce Lake to look for lost Jake Doxey. And, I suppose——"

What Mr. Bobbsey was going to say was lost in joyous shouts from Nan, Bert, Flossie and Freddie.

"Hurray! Hurray!" they cried. "We're going to Spruce Lake!"

Then, all of a sudden, from the kitchen was heard the voice of Dinah, who yelled:

"Snap! Snap! Git away from dar! Stop it! Oh, mah good land ob massy! Now look whut yo' has gone an' done! Mr. Bobbsey, come in heah, quick!"

CHAPTER IV

OFF TO SPRUCE LAKE

AT THE sound of Dinah's shouts Bert Bobbsey leaped out of his chair so quickly that he upset himself and went sprawling on the ground.

He was up in an instant, not in the least hurt, and he led his father in a race up the back steps into the kitchen.

From that room the voice of Dinah could still be heard, saying:

"Quit it, Snap! Git away from dem cookies!"

"Oh, Mother!" exclaimed Nan. "Our dog is after the church cookies!"

"This seems to be their unlucky day," sighed Mrs. Bobbsey. "First Freddie gives them a shower bath and then Snap tries to steal them."

"Come heah, everybody!" yelled Dinah.

"Snap! Snap! Down!" ordered Bert, getting a glimpse of his dog with his front paws on the kitchen table where the bundle of cookies had been placed. "Get down, Snap!"

Mrs. Bobbsey had followed her husband and the children up the back steps from the pleasant shade of the back yard under the grapevine where they had listened to the story of lost Jake Doxey. She looked in through the door as Bert and Mr. Bobbsey entered and saw Snap about to eat the cookies, as she thought.

"Oh, don't let him take those cakes!" she cried. "They are for the church supper and there is no time to make more. Oh, what a bad dog Snap is! I never knew him to do anything like that before."

"I didn't, either," said Nan. "Oh, Snap!"

By this time Bert and Mr. Bobbsey had reached the table, but there was no need to pull Snap away or do anything to stop him from eating the cookies. For Snap wasn't after the cookies, though Dinah thought he was when he rose up from the floor and put his front feet on the edge of the table.

"Look!" cried Bert as he patted his dog's head. "Snap was only after these little frogs. He thought they were going to spoil the cookies so he started to drive the frogs away."

"Frogs!" cried Mrs. Bobbsey, in surprise. "Frogs on the kitchen table! It can't be!"

"But look," said Bert, and, reaching out his hand, he picked up a good-sized green frog, one of several that were hopping about the table near the broken-open package of cookies.

"Oh, look at the frogs!" cried Freddie, who had followed the others into the kitchen. "Look! Look!"

"How did they get there?" asked Nan.

"Maybe the frogs came out of the cookies," said Flossie.

"Nonsense!" exclaimed Nan. "Bert and I got those cookies from Mrs. Porter's house and I'm sure she never put any frogs in."

"Of course she didn't," declared Bert.

"But here are frogs," said Mrs. Bobbsey, pointing at several of the green jumpers which Bert was catching as fast as he could, while Snap looked on eager to do his share. Only he didn't get a chance.

As for fat, black Dinah, she stared at the frogs in her kitchen with wide-open, popping eyes.

"It jes' can't be!" she said. "I mus' be asleep an' dreamin' 'bout it. Dey isn't frogs!"

"Yes, they are!" cried Freddie, picking one up. "And it's alive, too!" He held a frog by its hind legs out toward Flossie. Dinah picked up one, finding it real, and alive. Then she saw a small box on one end of the table, not far from the cookies. At the same time Sam Johnson, her husband, came shuffling in from the yard.

"Sam Johnson, am dese yo' frogs?" demanded Dinah, in rather an angry voice.

"Whut frogs?" asked Sam.

"Dese yeah frogs whut done nearly eat up Mrs. Bobbsey's church-sociable cookies," answered Dinah. "Am dey yo' frogs, Sam?"

"I dunno 'less I see 'em," he said cautiously.

"Well, am dis yo' fishin'-bait box?" asked Dinah, holding it up. It was a small box covered on one end with mosquito wire netting and had a strong, fishy smell.

"Yais, dat's mah fishin'-bait box," admitted Sam.

"An' did yo' hab frogs in it to go fishin'?" asked Dinah, while the Bobbsey family waited for what was to come next.

"Yais, I had some frogs," admitted Sam, looking at those in the hands of his wife, Bert and Flossie and Freddie, while one or two were still on the table. "I cotched 'em to use fo' bait an'——"

"Yais, an' yo' done lef' yo' bait box on mah kitchen table!" declared Dinah, her voice now loud. "An' de frogs done got out an' when Bert an' Nan left de church cookies on de table dem frogs smell 'em an' bust out ob yo' bait box an' if it hadn't been fo' dat good dog Snap all de cookies would 'a' been down inside de frogs by now."

"No," said Sam, shaking his head, "frogs don't eat cookies."

"How you know?" demanded his wife. "Dey'd spoil 'em, anyhow. Now, Sam Johnson, yo' take dem hoppin' frogs out ob mah kitchen or I'll neber gib yo' a bit of supper dis night. Get dem frogs out an' dat bait box, too, else I'll frow 'um to Kingdom Come."

"No, don't hurt de frogs!" begged Sam. "Dey's got to be alive fo' bait else they ain't no good. I'll take 'em away. I guess I mus' 'a' forgot an' left mah bait box on yo' table, Dinah."

"Hu!" muttered Dinah. "Yo' only guess yo forgot, does you? Well, I knows yo' forgot.

An' if yo' does it ag'in I'll do somethin' mo' dan jest talk! Now git dem frogs out!"

This, Sam was very glad to do. No harm had been done to the cookies, and Snap had not gone near them when he wandered in out of the yard and happened to see the frogs on the table. He was given a cookie as a reward and then the cakes were put away to be taken to the church later, ready for the supper that was to be given by Mrs. Bobbsey and other ladies.

"But, Mother," said Nan, a little later, when the excitement about the frogs was over and everything was quiet, with Dinah getting ready the evening meal, "you won't have time for any church supper if we are going to Spruce Lake."

"That's right," chimed in Bert. "When are we going, anyhow?"

"Oh, not for a few days," said Mr. Bobbsey. "Your mother will have time to sell those cookies at the church supper if there are any left after Freddie's fire-engine wetting and the frogs," he added, with a laugh.

"I didn't wet very many cookies," stated Freddie.

"And the frogs didn't eat any," added Bert. "Good old Snap was too quick for 'em."

"Snap is getting old," said Mrs. Bobbsey, "but he is still good to keep frogs from eating cookies."

"I'll frog dat Sam Johnson if he brings his fish-bait box in mah kitchen any mo'," muttered Dinah, as she came in to say that supper was now on the table.

After the meal the Bobbsey twins talked about nothing but going to Spruce Lake. They wanted to know all about it, where it was, how big it was, and how long they could stay.

Some of the questions, especially about the lake, Mr. Bobbsey could answer, for he had been up there more than once to look at the timberland. There were deep woods all around Spruce Lake, which got its name because there were so many spruce trees near it.

"But I can't tell how long we'll stay," he said. "I want to find Jake Doxey if I can. He's the only man I can do business with and I must find him so I can buy that timberland of him."

"How can you find him if he's lost?" asked Nan.

"Oh, I don't suppose he is really lost," her father explained; "that is, not lost so that he, himself, doesn't know where he is. I think he has just gone off into the woods where nobody lives and is having a quiet time hunting and fishing. He doesn't know I want to find him to buy his land or he would come out where I can talk to him. He has no reason for keeping hid. It's just a question of finding where he is so I can talk business with him."

"We'll help you look for him when we go to Spruce Lake," promised Freddie. "I'll show him my fire engine."

"And I'll show him my dolls," offered Flossie, not to let her twin brother get ahead of her.

"Pooh, a lumberman like Jake Doxey won't want to see dolls!" declared Freddie, with a sniff. "He'd rather look at my fire engine. Maybe, if the woods get on fire as they do sometimes, I can help put out the blaze with my engine," added the little boy. "It squirts a lot of water. Can't I, Daddy?"

"No, you can't," said Flossie. "The woods aren't going to get on fire, anyhow, are they, Daddy?"

"I hope not," was the answer. "But it is good to know that my little fireman will do his part if he has to."

"I'll let my dolls watch," declared blue-eyed Flossie.

"Is there any fishing in the lake?" asked Bert. He had a fine new rod that he had bought with the money Aunt Sallie Pry had given him for helping find the treasure.

"Oh, yes, there is good fishing in Spruce Lake," answered Mr. Bobbsey. "It is quite a camping-out place."

"Won't the camps all be closed by the time we get there?" Mrs. Bobbsey wanted to know.

"I think some campers will be left at the time we go up next week," said her husband. "I want to get hold of this timberland of Jake's as soon as I can to start cutting this winter. I think we shall have plenty of company up there."

"That will be fine," said Nan. "I'll take my new tennis racquet. Maybe there'll be a court there. I hope I'll meet some girls."

"You will," said her father.

"And I hope I'll find some fellows to go

fishing with," added Bert. "But, Daddy, how are we going—by train?"

"No, I think we'll travel by auto," was the answer. "It will be easier that way. It will take about two days and we can stop over the night at some hotel."

"Oh, I know it's going to be just grand!" exclaimed Nan. "But are you sure we'll not miss any school?" she asked anxiously, for she was doing well in her class and did not want to get behind.

"I think you won't miss any school," said her father. "I will find out for sure about that to-morrow."

The next day Mr. Bobbsey telephoned up from his lumberyard to his wife, saying to tell the children that school would be a month late in opening that fall.

"So we shall go to Spruce Lake at the end of this week," he added, and when the Bobbsey twins heard that they let out shouts of joy, and even Bert and Nan joined a little parade started by Flossie and Freddie who marched around the yard leading Snap by a string around his neck.

The next few days passed quickly and after

some packing was done and the house had been left in charge of Sam and Dinah, the family got in the big auto and started off. Mr. Bobbsey had heard nothing more about Jake Doxey, but hoped to find him somewhere in the woods around the lake.

"Here we go! Here we go!" chanted Freddie, as he lugged his fire engine, packed in a box, out of the house to put in the auto.

"Oh, what fun! Oh, what fun!" sang Flossie, hugging her doll Goldie.

Bert had his fishing rod and Nan took her tennis racquet and some books to read.

"All aboard!" called Mr. Bobbsey sitting at the steering wheel. "We're off!"

And off they started for Spruce Lake where they were to have many adventures.

CHAPTER V

A QUEER CATCH

Mrs. Bobbsey was trying to settle herself comfortably in the rear seat of the auto, where she sat with Flossie, Freddie and Nan. Bert was in the front place with his father, who was driving. But, somehow or other, Mrs. Bobbsey did not feel easy. She moved about this way and that way.

"What's the matter, Mother?" asked Nan, who was sitting beside her. Flossie and Freddie were on two extra seats right behind their father and Bert.

"This seat seems very hard," complained Mrs. Bobbsey. "I can't get any rest in it. It's just as if I were sitting on something round and hard."

"Maybe you're sitting on our sweaters," suggested Nan. "I put a bundle of sweaters in that corner of the seat near you."

"Yes, the sweaters are here," said Mrs. Bobbsey, remembering that she had told Nan to put them in the car in case it should get cool toward evening as they rode along, for they were in a touring car and not the sedan. "The sweaters are here all right," went on Nan's mother. "But there seems to be something hard in them. I'm sitting on it and it isn't comfortable."

She put her hand in among the sweaters and began feeling about. A moment later she brought out a large bottle of water which she held up, exclaiming:

"What's this?"

Freddie looked around from his seat in front of his mother and said:

"That's my bottle of water."

"Your bottle of water?" questioned Mrs. Bobbsey, with a laugh. "Did you think you would get thirsty on the way? If you should you could have a drink from the thermos bottle Bert has."

"Oh, I didn't put that bottle of water in to drink," explained Freddie, seriously enough. "It's for my fire engine to pump in case the woods get on fire. Don't throw it away!" he begged eagerly, as he saw his mother hold the bottle over the side of the moving car. "I want it for my engine."

"Oh, you and your engine!" said Nan. "The idea of making Mother sit on a hard bottle of water."

"I didn't know she was going to sit on it," Freddie defended himself truly enough. "And maybe I'll have to work my engine."

"You are a true fireman!" chuckled Mr. Bobbsey. "You are always ready, my boy. But I hardly think you will need to start your engine, so put the bottle of water away," he said to his wife.

"You might save it in case our engine gets hot and we could use it in the radiator," suggested Bert.

"Yes, that's so," agreed his father, "though a quart of water wouldn't go very far toward cooling off a hot radiator. But save it if you like," he added.

"I'll carry it," offered Freddie.

However, his mother knew that if she let him have the bottle of water up on his small seat he might drop it or spill the water, so she found a place for it on the floor at her feet among some valises where it rode safely.

The Bobbsey twins enjoyed the trip from the very start. The day was lovely, not too warm, and the road was a good one. For several miles the way lay along a road over which Bert and the others had often traveled, so there was nothing new to see. But the children were so delighted at the prospect before them of spending a month in the woods around Spruce Lake for an unexpected vacation, that they were happy over everything. They laughed when they saw a dog trotting along the road. They laughed when they saw a cat sitting on the steps of some farmhouse they passed.

Flossie and Freddie started to keep count of the horses and cows they passed, but as they were now out in the country they had to give it up as there were so many animals to be seen.

Freddie had a little puzzle that Bert had given him to play with and, after a while, when the small boy grew tired of looking at the sights along the way, he took out this puzzle and tried to work it. The trick was to get a ring loose from a tangle of wire to which it seemed fastened.

Flossie had her doll Goldie to take care of and, as the road was now getting dusty, Flossie decided she would put a veil around Goldie's head to keep her clean. The veil was a piece of mosquito netting but, as Flossie said, "It looks as real as anything, and just like lace."

Nan was talking to her mother, asking about the trip and where they would stay that night.

"We aren't going to sleep in this auto, are we?" Nan wanted to know.

"Indeed not!" laughed Mrs. Bobbsey. "I think your father plans to stop over night at some hotel."

"Oh, I love hotels!" exclaimed Nan. "It's so nice not to have to wash or dry the dishes after you get through eating."

"It would be a funny hotel," chuckled Bert, "where you had to wash and dry your own dishes."

"Do you wash the dishes at home, Nan?" asked her mother, and laughed a little.

"Well, I often help Dinah dry them when there's an extra lot, as when company comes," replied Nan. "And it isn't so much fun eating, even a company meal, when you know you have to dry the dishes afterward. That's why I like hotels, you don't have to worry about the dishes."

"That surely is one nice thing about hotels," admitted Mrs. Bobbsey. "Do you know where we are going to stop to-night, Dick?" she asked her husband, who had been talking to Bert about the new lumber tract it was hoped Jake Doxey would sell, if the missing man could be found.

"If all goes well we should be in Crescent Falls before dark," said Mr. Bobbsey, "and we'll stop at the hotel there. It's a good one. I have put up at it many times."

"I'm going to take my fire engine in the hotel with me," said Freddie, looking up from the ring puzzle. "I'm not going to leave it in this car in the garage. Somebody might take it."

"There will be no danger of that," his father said, "and your toy is too big to carry around and take up in the hotel bedroom, Freddie. I'll tell the garage man to keep special watch over our things during the night."

"Well, then, maybe it will be all right," Freddie said. "But I wouldn't want any one to take my engine that Aunt Sallie bought for me out of the treasure hunt."

"And I don't want anybody to take my doll," added Flossie.

"Pooh! Nobody wants dolls!" said Freddie.

"They do so!" cried Flossie. "Specially a doll like my Goldie. I'm going to take her to bed with me."

As the doll was not as large as Freddie's engine, Mrs. Bobbsey said Flossie might do this.

After riding along several miles and having asked as many questions as he could think of about Jake Doxey and where Mr. Bobbsey believed the missing man might be, Bert decided that he would look at his new fishing rod to make sure it was all right in the cloth bag which he used to protect it. He took out the three pieces, for it was a jointed rod, and began fitting them together, thrusting the long, slender end out from under the top of the touring car at his right.

Mr. Bobbsey was talking to his wife about what they might do when they reached Spruce Lake next day, so he did not pay much attention to what Bert was doing. And Bert, having made sure that the pole was all right, decided to put on the reel, with its layers of line, and see how it would run out of the little wire loop at the tip of the pole. So Bert strung his line through the guides on the pole and was wishing he had a place to fish when, all of a sudden, the reel, or nickeled wheel on which the cord was wound, began to buzz merrily.

"Sounds as if you'd caught a fish, Bert," said his father, turning to look at the boy beside him. "Why, you have caught something!" he added as he saw the bending pole which was thrust out one side of the car.

The reel kept on buzzing, and the line ran out. Bert did not know what to make of it. He was afraid his rod would break, for it was bending like a bow when his father put on the brakes and stopped the auto. Then Bert leaned out and looked back.

A loop of his line had caught on a tree branch as the car rolled past and, holding fast there, was paid out from the reel, causing that to turn and hum.

"Oh, you have caught a fish!" cried Freddie, as Bert began to turn the little handle of the reel and wind up his line.

"Ho! How could he catch a fish on dry land?" asked Flossie.

"Well, maybe he's caught a bird," Freddie said.

Though it was not a bird that had become tangled on Bert's line, it was the next thing to it. As he reeled in, on the end of the cord dangled part of a bird's nest.

"Oh, look!" cried Nan, as the mass of sticks, string, horsehair and feathers came nearer, fastened on the hookless end of Bert's fishing line. "What a funny catch!"

"It surely is," agreed Mr. Bobbsey. "How'd you get that, Bert?"

"The nest must have been built out on the end of a branch, and my pole and line tangled around it when we went under it," was the answer. "I didn't know the trees were so close."

"You shouldn't have had your rod sticking out so far," warned his mother. "It might have been broken."

"That's right," agreed Bert, as he reeled the dangling nest in where he could reach it and untangle it from his line.

"Oh, maybe there were little birds in the

nest and you dumped them out!" exclaimed Flossie.

"It is too late in the season for birds to be in nests," said Bert. "This was an old one. The birds flew away long ago."

"That's right," agreed Mr. Bobbsey. "Better take your rod apart now, Bert, and put it away."

"Yes," agreed the boy, "I guess I had. I'm glad it didn't break when it hit the tree."

So they journeyed on, talking and laughing among themselves. The twins were very eager to get to Spruce Lake where their fun would begin.

They stopped for lunch in a little country town, and though Freddie was very desirous of taking out his fire engine, put in the water from the bottle he had brought, and start the pump going to show the waiter at their table, his mother would not let him.

They went on again after lunch and were driving along a quiet country road when Bert, sitting beside his father, pointed ahead and cried suddenly:

"Look out, Dad!"

The road curved sharply here and coming

around the bend was an old, ramshackle junk wagon, drawn by a bony horse. On the seat was a man, but he was asleep and the horse was over on the wrong side of the road.

"Oh, we're going to smash into him!" cried Mrs. Bobbsey.

Freddie and Flossie were bouncing about on their seats and yelling:

"Oh, we're going to have a smash! We're going to have a smash!"

CHAPTER VI

A RUNAWAY BOY

MR. BOBBSEY was a good and careful auto driver. As soon as he saw the junk wagon, with the man asleep on the seat and not guiding the ambling horse, Mr. Bobbsey knew that he must steer to the left instead of keeping to the right.

Of course when passing other autos or wagons coming toward you it is the rule of the road to keep to the right. But when others are wrong it is sometimes best to go wrong yourself and so keep out of danger.

"Hold fast, everybody!" called Mr. Bobbsey to his family. "I may clear him or there may be a smash. But hold tight, anyhow."

So Bert, Nan and all the others held on as best they could so they would not be bounced out of their seats in case of a collision.

However, Mr. Bobbsey was going to do his best not to have a smash.

At this curve of the road, where the junk wagon had been met, there was a high bank on one side and on the other side a smaller bank with a little brook along it. The high bank was on Mr. Bobbsey's left and he now turned toward that, hoping there was room for him to drive the big car between the hill of grass and dirt and the junk wagon.

There was room, but only just enough, and when the junkman's horse saw the big car so close to him, the animal took fright and turned farther toward the left side of the road—the side where the brook was running.

The horse turned sharply, started up over the low bank and gave the wagon such a twist that it turned over on its side and spilled everything out that was in it.

There was more in that wagon than the Bobbsey twins at first believed. They could see the sleeping man on the seat suddenly thrown off and go flying through the air, finally sprawling out on the soft grass beside the brook. That woke him up, let me tell you!

In the wagon were bundles of old newspapers, a lot of worn automobile tires, part of a cook stove, some other pieces of iron and an old bed mattress. All this stuff was tossed out and scattered over the small bank, some of the things rolling down into the brook. Mostly the junk wagon was filled with bundles of old newspapers, and some of these were quite large, almost as tall as Bert or Nan.

"Whew!" exclaimed Mr. Bobbsey, as he brought his auto to a stop beyond the big side hill at his left. "That was a close shave!"

"Did you bump him?" asked Mrs. Bobbsey, her heart not beating so fast now that she saw her family was safe.

"No, I never so much as scraped the hubs of his wheels," said Mr. Bobbsey. "The horse turned too suddenly. That's what sent the wagon down over the little bank."

"Oh, I hope he isn't hurt!" murmured Mrs. Bobbsey, looking at the junkman, who, though now awake, was still sprawled at the side of the brook in the soft grass.

"No, he isn't hurt," said Bert. "He's getting up."

This the junkman was doing, but there was

a look of great surprise on his face. He looked at his wagon, turned on one side, at the bundles of paper and other trash scattered all over, and then at his horse which had broken loose from the shafts. The animal had not run away. Perhaps it was too old and bony to do anything like that. Anyhow, it was now quietly eating grass beside the road.

"I guess it's glad of a chance to get a meal," said Mrs. Bobbsey.

As for the junkman, after looking around him, he glanced up, saw the big touring car beside the road, and noticed Mr. Bobbsey and Bert getting out of it and walking toward him.

"What alla de matter?" asked the junkman, who was an Italian.

"You were asleep and let your horse wander on the wrong side of the road," said Mr. Bobbsey, and his voice showed anger. "I almost ran into you. What do you mean by going to sleep when you're driving a horse?"

"Excusa me," said the man, walking around and looking about him in a dazed way. He didn't yet quite know what had happened. "I upa late lasta da night. Mebby I sleep."

"No maybe about it," said Mr. Bobbsey sternly. "If I hadn't turned quickly I'd have smashed right into you. Are you hurt?"

"No, t'anks. Nota much," and he began to feel of his arms and legs. None was broken, and aside from being a bit dusty and somewhat wet from having gone partly into the brook, he was all right. "Alla my stuff spoil," he complained.

"Well, it's your own fault," said Mr. Bobbsey. "You had no right to go to sleep."

"Poor man," murmured Mrs. Bobbsey kindly. "He didn't mean to do it Dick."

"No, I suppose not, and I'll help him gather up his stuff. He hasn't lost anything and you can't hurt junk just by upsetting it."

By this time the man had seen that his piles of papers, his old tires, the mattress and the iron were not in the least harmed, though things were pretty well scattered along the road and over the bank. So he took heart, especially when he saw that his wagon, though turned over, was not broken and his horse had not run away and was not even scratched.

"I mucha sorry," he said, reaching up his hand to take off his ragged hat to bow to Mrs.

Bobbsey. But the hat was some distance off lying on the edge of the brook.

"Come along. I'll help you right your wagon and pick up some of your stuff," offered Mr. Bobbsey. "You're lucky to be no worse off. After this keep awake when you're driving along the road."

"Sure, I will," the man promised. "I mucha glad you no smash into me. I got busted once, longa time ago, worse dan dis. Come here, Rosita," he called to his horse. "No eata too mucha de grass—you geta seek."

"Isn't he funny!" whispered Flossie to her mother.

By this time Bert and Nan had walked over to where several big bundles of papers were tilted together on the edge of the brook. Bert was going to roll them to a place where the junkman could more easily lift them into his wagon when it should have been righted. But Nan, suddenly pointing between two bundles, cried:

"Look, Bert!"

"What is it?" he asked.

"A boy! In those paper bundles!" exclaimed Nan.

As she spoke and pointed, Bert and the others saw a boy crawling out from amid the papers. It seemed such a surprising sight that the children did not know what to say.

The boy himself seemed surprised. He rubbed one elbow and then his head as if he had been bumped in the upset, but he did not seem to have been hurt.

He was, perhaps, a little older than Bert, and did not seem at all the kind of a boy who would belong to a junkman or even working on a junk wagon. With the surprise shown on the boy's face there was also a hard look as if he were angry.

"Hello," said Bert, in friendly greeting.

"Hello yourself," answered the boy, and his voice did not seem to be friendly.

"Hallo!" added the junkman, walking over, as did Mr. Bobbsey, toward the pile of papers and the strange boy. "Where youa come from?"

"Out of your wagon," was the answer. The boy began to straighten out his clothes which were rumpled and mussed. He was as well dressed as was Bert Bobbsey.

"You coma outa da wagon?" asked the

junkman, in surprise. "How youa git in my wagon?"

"I sneaked in when you stopped at the last place where you picked up those old tires," and the boy pointed to several scattered about. "I hid down in the bundles of paper and I guess I went to sleep. Next thing I knew I felt myself shooting through the air and I crawled out. What happened?"

"We nearly ran into him," explained Bert.

"What, have you got a junk wagon, too?" asked the strange boy.

"We were in that car," explained Bert, with a smile, pointing to the auto drawn up near the opposite bank. "This man was asleep, too, and on the wrong side of the road."

"Oh, so that's how it happened," went on the strange boy. "Did you hit him hard?"

"We didn't hit him at all," answered Bert, while Mr. Bobbsey and the others, the junkman included, listened. "His horse swung the wagon over the bank by the brook and the wagon upset. That's how you and the papers were dumped out."

"Oh, so that's how it was!" murmured the boy. "Well, I'm glad it was no worse. I'll give you a hand picking up your stuff if you'll let me keep on riding with you," he added to the Italian.

"Sure," was the answer. "Wherea you go?"

"Don't know," the boy replied shortly.

"Don't you know where you're going?" asked Bert, in surprise.

"No. I'm running away from home and I don't care where I go," was the sharp answer.

The Bobbsey twins looked at one another in wonder.

CHAPTER VII

AT CRESCENT FALLS

MR. BOBBSEY, who had started to help the junkman turn the upset wagon rightside up, stopped as he heard what the strange boy had said. Thinking he might not have heard aright, Mr. Bobbsey asked him:

"What did you say you were doing in those bundles of papers?"

"I was hiding—sneaking a ride. I'm running away from home," was the answer, and the boy did not speak pleasantly or politely.

"Running away! What for?" asked Bert's father.

"Because I don't like it at home," the boy said sullenly. He kept his eyes looking at the ground and seemed trying to dig a little pit with his feet.

"What's wrong at home?" Mrs. Bobbsey asked.

"I had a quarrel with my father," was the reply. "He said he was going to lick me. So I ran away."

"Do you think that was a good thing to do?" asked Mrs. Bobbsey, and her voice was low and gentle.

"Well, it wasn't a good thing for my father to say he was going to lick me," muttered the boy. "I'm too big to be licked."

"Perhaps you are," said Mr. Bobbsey quietly. "But maybe you did something that you should be punished for."

"I didn't do much," said the boy. "Somebody told my father things that weren't true about me. It wasn't fair. But I won't stand being licked. If he ever does that I'll run away and never go back."

"But look here, my boy—what's your name?" asked Mr. Bobbsey suddenly.

"Frank Denton."

"Where do you live?"

"In Crescent Falls."

"Why, that's where we're going!" exclaimed Freddie. "And when we get there I'll show you my fire engine. It squirts real water."

"If you squirt any more on me or my dolls

I'll never speak to you again, Freddie Bobb-sey!" said Flossie, remembering what had happened on the porch the day Bert and Nan had reached home with the cookies.

"Hush, dear," whispered Mrs. Bobbsey, for Mr. Bobbsey wanted to talk more to the run-away boy.

"So you live in Crescent Falls," Mr. Bobbsey went on. "I know some people there but I don't know any Mr. Denton."

"We haven't lived there long," Frank ex-plained. "But I'm not going to live there at all if my father doesn't act differently."

"Now look here," said Mr. Bobbsey, going close to the sullen boy and putting a hand kindly on his shoulder, "let's talk about this. You say some one told your father things about you that weren't so, Frank?"

"That's what they did."

"Well, suppose some one told you things about your father that weren't true. Wouldn't you want to hear his side of the story and find out the truth?"

"Yes, I guess maybe I would."

"And wouldn't you be glad if your father, instead of going off by himself angrily, came to you and talked about it—wouldn't you?"

"I—I guess so."

"Well, then, why don't you go back home and tell your father the truth? Explain just what happened, and I'm sure he will never punish you for something you didn't do. Isn't he fair toward you?"

"Sometimes—yes."

"I'm sure he will be again. Now we are going on to Crescent Falls and we shall be glad to give you a ride home in our car. We have room and you will be quite welcome. Will you ride with us?"

The boy seemed to be thinking it over. He was still sullen and angry and not yet ready to give in. Then up spoke Freddie.

"I'll show you my fire engine," he said.

A trace of a smile showed around the corners of Frank Denton's mouth. Before he could answer Flossie piped up with:

"And I'll let you hold my doll."

"Pooh!" cried Freddie. "Boys don't want to hold dolls."

"Hush, my dears," whispered their mother.

"Better come with us," urged Bert, as one

boy to another. "I have a dandy new fishing rod."

Whether it was that or the prospect of seeing Freddie's fire engine in action no one knew, but the runaway boy suddenly looked up at Mr. Bobbsey, smiled a little, and said:

"All right. Thanks! I'll ride back home with you."

"That's good. I'm sure you won't be sorry you went back to your father and explained things," said the lumber merchant. "Now we must help this poor man get straightened out and then we'll travel along."

"It was his own fault he got his wagon tipped over, wasn't it?" asked Frank. "Let him fix things up himself."

"No, we must help," said Mr. Bobbsey, and Bert looked sharply at the runaway boy. He seemed rather mean, Bert thought, especially after he had ridden in among the junkman's papers, stealing a ride.

But Frank helped Mr. Bobbsey and the Italian and the wagon was soon turned over on its wheels and pulled out on the road, this time on the right side. It was a light wagon and the two boys and Mr. Bobbsey easily managed it. I should say three boys, for Freddie insisted on pulling and hauling with the others, though his mother was afraid he would get in the way and be hurt. But he wasn't.

Then came the work of picking up the bits of scattered junk and putting them back in the wagon. Most of this work Mr. Bobbsey and the boys left for the Italian to do, as he had plenty of time and knew best how he wanted it stowed on his wagon. The old, bony horse did not wander away but kept on eating grass until it was once more hitched between the shafts.

"Good-bye!" called Mr. Bobbsey to the junkman, when the auto party, with the addition of Frank Denton as company, was ready to travel on again.

"Oh, gooda-bye!" was the reply, with a wave of a brown hand. "Mucha thanka! I no go sleep any more on da wagon."

"No, it isn't safe," chuckled the lumber dealer. "And keep your horse on the right side of the road."

"Sure, boss!" was the answer, and they left him still picking up bundles of papers.

"Where do you live in Crescent Falls, Frank?" asked Mr. Bobbsey, as he looked at the lad sitting on the outer edge of the front seat next to Bert.

"On a street where there's a hardware store on the corner, if you know where that is," was the answer.

"Oh, yes, I know Mr. Blake's hardware store," said Mr. Bobbsey. "I have sold him lumber. I have been in Crescent Falls before. That street is on our way to the hotel and we can leave you at your house."

"Thanks," said Frank, and his voice was still sullen and he did not seem very happy at going back home. Mrs. Bobbsey felt sorry for him. She thought there must be something wrong, somewhere.

It was not such a jolly party of Bobbsey twins that was now traveling along, for Frank did not join in the talk and he seemed sullen and glum. Bert tried several times to get him to talk, but it was not of much use. So they were all, except perhaps Flossie and Freddie who never seemed to worry about anything, rather glad when at last Crescent Falls was reached.

This was a small town about halfway between Spruce Lake and Lakeport where Mr. Bobbsey intended to put his family up at a hotel over night. It was now late afternoon and the weather seemed to be clouding up.

"I hope it will not rain to-morrow," said Mrs. Bobbsey, as they drove on through the town.

"If it rains I can get a lot of water for my fire engine," said Freddie, with a laugh.

"I don't want it to rain," declared Flossie. "I haven't any waterproof for Goldie."

"As traveling in the rain is no fun, I hope, with you, my dear, that it is clear to-morrow," said Mrs. Bobbsey, giving Flossie a hug.

After a little while Frank Denton spoke and said:

"This is my street. I live the fifth house up on the right."

"Then we'll stop there," said Mr. Bobbsey with a smile, as he turned the corner at the hardware store. "Here you are!" he added, when the car had come to a stop in front of a brown house.

A worried-looking woman, who had been

peering up and down the street as the Bobbsey auto drew near, now hurried to the sidewalk as Frank got out.

"Oh, Frank!" exclaimed his mother. "I've been so worried! I've been looking all over for you. Where have you been?"

"I ran away," was the answer, and Bert was surprised that the boy should thus speak out so boldly.

"Ran away?" repeated his mother.

"Yes, on a junk wagon. And Mr. Bobbsey, here, ran into the wagon, or he almost did, and it was upset and I got chucked out and he offered to bring me back. So here I am."

"Well, Frank, I'm certainly glad to see you," said his mother. "But why did you run away?"

"Because Pa said he was going to lick me. I won't stand being licked by him. If he tries it again I'll run away once more and stay for good."

"Oh, dear!" sighed Mrs. Denton, as Frank shuffled into the house, pausing only long enough to mutter over his shoulder to Mr. Bobbsey:

"Thanks! Good-bye!"

"I feel so sorry for your son," said Mrs.

Bobbsey as the woman came out to the curb. "He seems to be in trouble."

. "He and his father don't get along very well," was the answer. "Frank is very wild, I'm sorry to say. He doesn't always do as he should. This makes his father mad. He has quite a temper."

"Is Mr. Denton at home now?" asked Mr. Bobbsey, thinking perhaps he might say a good word for Frank and ask that he be given more gentle treatment.

"No, he isn't," answered Mrs. Denton. "He's away on business. He went early this morning after he and Frank had words. It must have been after that that Frank decided to run away. I'm glad he didn't run far. I hope this will be a lesson to him. I'm so worried about him. Was anybody hurt when you ran into the junk wagon?"

"We didn't exactly run into it," explained Mrs. Bobbsey, telling how the accident happened. "And your son wasn't hurt. He seems like a nice boy, only perhaps he doesn't understand his father and his father doesn't understand him. Things are that way sometimes."

"Yes," agreed Mrs. Denton. "It's just

as well my husband isn't at home now. For if he heard Frank had run away there would be more trouble. I must try and patch it up as best I can. I'm much obliged to you for bringing my son home."

"You are quite welcome," answered Mr. Bobbsey. "We are going on to Spruce Lake in the morning, and we may see your son again."

"No, he never goes there," said the woman. "I guess you won't meet him again unless you come here."

Having said good-bye to Mrs. Denton, the Bobbseys drove on through the town of Crescent Falls and finally reached the Mansion House, where they were to stay for the night.

"But where is the waterfall?" said Flossie who had heard talk about it several times that day.

"Just back of the hotel," answered Mr. Bobbsey. "You can hear the roar of the water when you get upstairs to your rooms, perhaps. Well, here is where we get out," and he slowly drove the car up in front of the hotel from which came a porter to help unload the bags.

"I'll drive the car around to the garage and be back with you in a few minutes," said Mr.

Bobbsey as he handed the valises to the porter
to take in. "Just wait for me in the lobby," he
added to his wife.

She led the children into the hotel, another
porter coming out to help the first, as there
were a number of bags. Mr. Bobbsey had
started to drive the car to the hotel garage
around the corner when Freddie set up a shout
and dashed back toward the street and in the
direction his father had taken.

"Here, what's the idea?" asked Bert in sur
prise.

"I want to get my fire engine!" cried Freddie
"My engine's in the auto."

"Well, leave it there," said Bert. "It will be
all right and you don't want it to-night."

"Yes, I do! I want it right now! There's a
fire! Look! I want to put it out!"

Freddie pointed to some paper blazing at
the edge of the hotel veranda.

"Dad! Dad! Stop! Let me get my engine and
put out the fire!" shouted Freddie

CHAPTER VIII

A FIERCE STORM

Freddie Bobbsey might easily have put out the little fire of paper on the hotel veranda with his toy engine, only some one else got ahead of him. A man who was sitting in a chair near the small blaze saw it about the same time Freddie did.

"Hello!" exclaimed the man in surprise. "I guess I'll have to be the fireman."

With that he stepped with one of his large feet on the piece of blazing paper and it went out in a puff of smoke. No harm was done, and it was all over in a few seconds.

So, as has been said, Freddie might have put out the fire, only the man got ahead of him and poor Freddie, who had rushed back toward his father's auto to get his engine, was sadly disappointed.

"Oh, dear!" he sighed in such a doleful way that the man asked:

"What's the matter, little man? Did you want to see the fire get so big that the hotel would burn down?"

"Oh, no, I didn't want that!" Freddie said, quickly enough. "I wanted to put the fire out myself with my own engine."

"Your engine!" exclaimed the man, with a smile, while Mrs. Bobbsey, Nan, Bert and Flossie listened. "Where is your engine?"

"In there," and Freddie pointed to the car. His father, seeing there was no danger, had started the auto again to drive it to the hotel garage around the corner. "I have a dandy little fire engine," Freddie went on. "Course it's a toy one," he explained, "but it has a hose and a pump and everything and it squirts real water."

"Is that so?" asked the man, who seemed fond of children. "But your engine can't be loaded with water when it's in your father's auto, can it?"

"Oh, I have a bottle of water all ready to put in the tank," explained Freddie. "I wish you'd a' let me put out the fire," he sighed.

"I will the next time," chuckled the man. "I didn't know we had a toy fire department so near. I guess some one must have thrown a lighted match down on that piece of paper," he said to several men who had gathered on the hotel porch. "Well, it's all over now and no harm done."

"Yes," said Freddie, with another sigh, "it's all out now. I can't use my engine."

"Never mind," put in Nan, who was leading Flossie into the hotel. "You can have fun with your engine when we get to Spruce Lake."

"I will, too!" declared the little fellow. "I'll put out a forest fire."

Flossie was cuddling Goldie, and as she walked on with Nan, the others of the Bobbsey family following, Flossie said:

"Did you get scared, my dear, when you saw the fire? Never mind, Mother will take care of you." Flossie felt that she was a real mother to each of her dolls.

"Pooh!" murmured Freddie. "Dolls can't get scared. She didn't even see the fire."

"She did so!" declared Flossie. "Goldie can see as good as you can, Freddie Bobbsey, or as good as your old fire engine can squirt."

"She can not!"

"She can so!"

"That will do, children," said Mrs. Bobbsey in a voice the two small twins knew they must obey. Flossie and Freddie often had little disputes about their toys, but their quarrels never lasted long. So now they were soon walking peaceably along together through the lobby of the hotel. Mr. Bobbsey came in a few minutes later, having put the car away. Then he registered all their names in the big book and a bellboy showed the family up to their rooms, taking them up in an elevator.

"I wish this was a big, high hotel," said Freddie in a low voice as the elevator stopped at the third floor.

"Why?" asked Bert, who was helping his mother carry some of her bundles, for they were too many for the bellboy to manage with all the valises. "Why do you want the hotel to be high?"

"So I could have a longer ride in the elevator," Freddie answered. "But maybe I can ride up and down a lot of times while we're here and that will do just as well."

They were soon in their rooms, Mr. and Mrs.

Bobbsey having one, Bert and Freddie another and Flossie and Nan being together in a room next to the one in which their father and mother were to stay.

The Bobbsey family was soon ready to go down to the evening meal. It was nothing new for the twins to eat in hotels, though they never quite got over the little thrill of sitting in a brightly lighted dining room, having waiters gliding about them, while from behind some green palms sounded soft music.

At first Mrs. Bobbsey wondered how such a small hotel as the Mansion House in Crescent Falls could have such a good orchestra as seemed to be playing the music. But a little later a man's voice sounded, stating that the music was coming from a big city broadcasting station miles away. That explained it.

After the meal Bert and Nan took Flossie and Freddie for a walk around the hotel square in the evening, where the children enjoyed the lively scenes. Then it was time to go back and get ready for bed.

Bert was getting out his pajamas and Freddie's and looking for his own toothbrush and his brother's when he noticed that Freddie was not in the room. Thinking he might have gone in to talk to Nan and Flossie or into Mr. and Mrs. Bobbsey's room farther down the hall, Bert went to look. But Freddie was in neither place.

"What are you looking for, Bert?" asked Mrs. Bobbsey.

"For Freddie," he answered. "He slipped out of our room."

"I hope he isn't lost," said Mrs. Bobbsey.

"Like Jake Doxey," added Mr. Bobbsey, with a smile. "He can't have gone far. I'll find Freddie."

He and Bert went out into the hall and they soon heard laughing from near the elevator. A colored boy's voice was saying:

"Ah t'ink yo' done ride enough now, little man."

"Oh, just once more up and down!" pleaded Freddie, and the secret was out.

Freddie had slipped away from Bert and had been riding up and down in the elevator, taking trip after trip to make up for the hotel not being high enough to give him a long ride all at once.

"Come now, Freddie, you've had plenty," his father said, trying not to laugh. "You shouldn't have done this."

"Oh, he's all right, suh," spoke up the colored elevator boy. "Ah don't mind him, but I was gittin' 'fraid mebby so much upin' and downin' might make him sick."

"No, it wouldn't, thank you," Freddie assured him. "I'd like more."

"Well, you've had enough," his father said. "Come on."

So Freddie went in with Bert to go to bed.

That's about all that happened to the Bobbsey twins in the hotel that night, except, that before Nan and Flossie were quite ready to go to bed a tap came on their door. Opening it, Nan saw a maid who asked:

"Did you ring, Miss?"

"Oh, no, thank you," Nan answered. "We don't need anything. But perhaps Mother rang."

"I'll go see," said the maid, as she closed the door.

Another tap soon came and another maid appeared with a pitcher of ice water.

"You rang for this," she said, with a smile.

"Oh, no, thank you, I didn't," Nan answered. "It must have been my mother."

"No, I rang the bell!" exclaimed Flossie quickly. "There!" she pointed to the wall where there were some electric push buttons, one to bring the chambermaid, another to bring some one with ice water, and a third which would summon the tailor to press the clothes of gentlemen guests.

"Flossie Bobbsey!" exclaimed Nan, in surprise. "What in the world did you do that for?"

"'Cause I wanted a drink for Goldie and me," explained the little girl.

"Oh, it's all right, Miss," said the maid, smiling. "We often bring up ice water. I'll set it on the stand for you," which she did, going out and closing the door.

"I hope Freddie doesn't get to ringing all the bells," thought Nan to herself, as she began to get ready for bed.

Next morning at breakfast Mr. Bobbsey said:

"I heard some good news a little while ago."

"Is it about Jake Doxey?" asked Bert.

"No," Mr. Bobbsey replied. "But I was talking to one of the men around the hotel, the one that put out the little paper fire last night," he said to his wife, "and he told me there is a large camp on Spruce Lake where they take boarders. I was thinking we might put up there and save the work of making a camp for ourselves."

"It sounds nice," said Mrs. Bobbsey. "What sort of camp is it, Dick?"

"One with a number of bungalows and cottages and a central dining room where meals are served. It will be a rest for you if you don't have to think of meals, now that you haven't Dinah."

"Yes, it would be lovely," agreed his wife.

"Oh, do let's live in the camp!" begged Bert.

"We could have a lot of fun," said Nan.

"Do you think I could get a boat for fishing?" Bert wanted to know.

"I think so," his father said. "Then it's settled. We'll take quarters in the Spruce Lake Camp. I'll telephone up and have them save a bungalow for us. Though I don't imagine they'll be crowded now, as it is near the end of the season."

Soon after breakfast Mr. Bobbsey did this, getting word over the telephone that there was a large bungalow for rent. He engaged it.

"The camp manager tells me," said Mr. Bobbsey coming back to tell his wife about the matter, "that there is still quite a crowd of campers there, with their children. The season is lasting longer this year."

"That's good," said Mrs. Bobbsey. "The children will have company."

The Bobbsey car was brought around from the garage and once more the family went journeying along toward Spruce Lake where they expected to arrive by nightfall.

But about halfway there they reached a place where a new road was being made and they had to take a detour which made traveling slow. In addition to this, the weather began to cloud up and the distant rumble of thunder was soon heard while the gathering darkness was set agleam by flashes of lightning.

"I don't like this," said Mr. Bobbsey to his wife, who was riding in the front seat with him, Bert being in the back one with Nan and the smaller twins.

"What don't you like?" she asked.

"This road we're on with a storm coming up. And I'm afraid the storm's going to be a bad one."

Hardly had Mr. Bobbsey spoken than it grew much darker and the rain came down swiftly. The thunder increased into a great rumble and roar and the flashes of lightning came oftener and became sharper. Once it seemed as if a tree near the Bobbseys was struck, so terrible was the crash.

"We can't keep on this way," said Mrs. Bobbsey, as the rain came down in such a gust of wind that Mr. Bobbsey could see only a few feet ahead. "Isn't there some place we could go for shelter, Dick?"

"I don't know this road," her husband answered. "I wish we could find a place."

"Look! Look!" suddenly called Freddie.

CHAPTER IX

ALARMED by Freddie's shout and thinking something had happened, Mr. Bobbsey put on the brakes and, peering ahead as well as he could through the rain, called out:

"What's the matter?"

"There's a barn!" Freddie answered. "It's a big barn and the doors are open and we can go in there. I'm getting all wet!"

Though there was a top to the auto, the side curtains were not up, and so suddenly had the storm gathered that there had been no time to put them in place. So the wind, sweeping the rain over the car, was wetting them all more or less.

"That's right, there is a barn," said Bert. "Over to your left, Daddy!"

In a moment Mr. Bobbsey saw the shelter. Freddie's sharp eyes had noticed it first. Perhaps Mr. Bobbsey might have seen it a moment later. But he was looking straight ahead.

"Yes, do drive in there," said Mrs. Bobbsey. "It will be some sort of shelter at least and this storm is getting worse every minute. Is there a road up to the barn, Dick?"

"Yes. It's a sort of cow lane, I judge, but I can make it. I don't know what the farmer will say to have us driving an auto into his barn, but here goes!" Mr. Bobbsey went on.

"Oh, he won't mind, I'm sure," his wife said.

"Maybe he's lonesome and he'll be glad to see us," said Flossie, who was trying to hold her doll away from the showers of raindrops that were whipped into her own face by the strong wind.

"There must be a house somewhere around to go with the barn," remarked Mr. Bobbsey, as he started up the car again and headed off the rough detour road toward the lane that led to the big, open building.

"There's a house a little farther down the highway," said Mrs. Bobbsey. "I had just a glimpse of it when the rain slackened for a moment. If this storm keeps up we can't go on to Spruce Lake," she remarked.

"No," her husband agreed. "Not over this road, anyhow, and I don't know of any other. Well, we'll be under shelter here, at least."

The barn floor was level with the lane and in another moment the auto, containing the Bobbsey family, was within the place. There was a sort of drive right through the barn, with big mows, or spaces, filled with fragrant hay on either side. The front doors were open but the back ones were closed, and, as the wind and rain came from the back, the children, with their father and mother, were soon in a well sheltered place. They could still hear the rumble of thunder and see the lightning, and the patter of rain on the roof was like the beating of many drums. But they were out of the storm.

"Thank goodness we're in here," said Mrs. Bobbsey, with a sigh of relief. "It's a terrible storm."

A quarter of an hour passed. The thunder and lightning were not quite so bad as at first, but the rain still kept up as hard as ever. And, remembering the bad state of the road, Mr. Bobbsey did not see how he could keep on over it in the auto.

"We'll get stuck in the mud, sure," he said.

While he and his wife were talking, trying to decide what was best to do, and while the children were looking about the barn to see what was to be seen, a man came in through the big, open doors through which Mr. Bobbsey had driven the car.

"Storm caught you folks, I reckon," said the man in a pleasant voice. "I saw you drive in. That detour is in bad shape."

"Yes, I took the liberty of driving into your barn, Mr.—er—Mr.——" the children's father did not know what name to use, as the farmer was a stranger.

"I'm Hiram Wardell," said the man, holding out his hand.. "You're welcome to stay as long as you like, but not here."

"Not here?" asked Mrs. Bobbsey, in surprise. She hoped the farmer was not going to make them go out into the storm again.

"Why, no. Come on up to the house," he said. "This is no place to stay. The house isn't far and if the children and you folks put some horse blankets over your heads you won't get very wet."

"Thank you," said Mr. Bobbsey.

"We have raincoats and umbrellas in the car," said Mrs. Bobbsey, "but it will be rather hard to get them out."

"Won't need to," said Mr. Wardell. "Horse blankets will do as well. Come along now. My folks are anxious to see you."

"It is very kind of you," said Mrs. Bobbsey. "But your wife may not like to have a lot of wet and muddy strangers tramping into her clean house."

"Oh, shucks!" laughed the farmer. "Come along and welcome. We get sort of lonesome living on this back road. It's been rather good since they put the detour through, for we've seen more cars in the past week than in a month of other times. My children will be glad to meet yours," he added. "Come along. I'll get some blankets."

He went into the lower part of the barn, coming back soon with some blankets, one for each member of the Bobbsey family. The farmer himself wore a yellow raincoat, or "slicker," and so kept dry.

The blankets were rather long for Flossie and Freddie and had to be doubled. But they made good protection and, as the farmer said.

his house was not far away. But the rain showed no sign of slacking and Mr. Bobbsey was wondering how he could keep on to Spruce Lake over such a bad road.

"Shall I take in my fire engine?" whispered Freddie to his mother, as they were about to start out, each one with a blanket.

"Goodness no!" she answered. "If you tried to carry that, your blanket would slip off and you'd get soaked."

"All right. I'll come out and get it after the rain stops and I'll make it squirt for the children up in the farmhouse," Freddie said.

"There's been enough water spilled this afternoon without you working your fire engine," chuckled Bert.

"That's right," his father said.

A quick dash down and across the road through the rain brought them to the farmhouse, where they were welcomed by Mrs. Wardell and a boy and girl, about the age of Nan and Bert. The children were named Charlie and Lena.

Mr. Bobbsey told Mr. and Mrs. Wardell who he was and spoke about going on to Spruce Lake to camp out.

"Isn't it rather late to begin camping?" asked the farmer, as his wife brought in some plates of molasses cookies and glasses of milk for the children.

"I'm not going there merely to camp," answered Mr. Bobbsey. "I want to buy a lumber tract; but the man who owns it is missing and I'm trying to locate him."

"What man is that?" asked the farmer.

"Jake Doxey," answered the lumber dealer.

"Jake Doxey! Why, I know him," said Mr. Wardell.

"You do?" asked Mr. Bobbsey eagerly. "Where is he? Is he around here? It will be a good thing for me if I can find him. Tell me about Jake Doxey."

CHAPTER X

FLAT ROCK CAMP

Nan and Bert Bobbsey were so interested in hearing what their father and Mr. Wardell had to say about the lost Jake Doxey that they forgot to eat their cookies and drink the rich, creamy milk. Flossie and Freddie, however, paid less attention to what the older folks were talking about, and went on with their lunch while Charlie and Lena looked curiously at the new children and the rain splashed down outside.

But it was cosy and snug in the big farm-house.

"I want to find Jake Doxey very much," went on Mr. Bobbsey.

"I'm afraid I can't tell you exactly where to find him," replied the farmer. "But some weeks ago he passed along this road and I spoke to him. He said he was going to camp out at the upper end of Spruce Lake."

"Just where we are going!" exclaimed Bert.

"Well, from what your father said," remarked Mr. Wardell, "you are going to camp near Flat Rock. That's at the lower end of the lake, and Jake said he was going toward the upper end. It's very wild up there."

"Are there wild animals?" eagerly asked Freddie, taking the glass of milk down from his lips long enough to ask this.

"Yes, there are some wild animals at the far end of Spruce Lake," said the farmer.

"Wolves?" asked Flossie, opening her blue eyes wide.

"Bears?" asked Freddie, taking another cookie.

"Lions?" was Flossie's next suggestion, while Freddie added:

"Tigers?"

"No, I wouldn't say there were any animals as wild as those up there," chuckled the farmer. "Nothing worse than foxes or maybe a bobcat or two, and even they won't bother you."

"Maybe I ought to have brought a gun instead of my fire engine," said Freddie, looking

around to make sure the doors and windows
were all well fastened.

"Nonsense!" exclaimed his mother. "And
don't let me catch you wandering off into the
woods to hunt make-believe wild animals,
either," she warned Freddie. "I don't want you
to get lost."

"Like Jake Doxey," said Nan, with a smile.

"You can't hunt make-believe wild animals," declared Freddie. "They have to be
real, else you can't shoot 'em!"

"Well, you stay around camp after we get
there," cautioned Mrs. Bobbsey. "Though if
this rain keeps up," she went on, as she glanced
toward the darkening windows, "I don't see
how we are going to get to Spruce Lake to-
day."

"You can't—not on that detour road," said
the farmer. "You folks had better stay here
all night."

"Oh, we couldn't think of that!" exclaimed
Mrs. Bobbsey. "It would put you out too
much."

"Not to be thought of," added Mr. Bobbsey,
"though we thank you for the offer. If there is
a hotel around here we can put up at that, for

night is coming on and the storm doesn't seem to be stopping. I don't like driving over a strange road after dark in a heavy rain like this."

"It wouldn't be safe," said Mr. Wardell. "As for stopping at a hotel, the nearest one of any account is in Crescent Falls."

"We just came from there," said Bert.

"And I rode up and down in the lelevators," Freddie said, giving the "lifts" a new name.

"And I rang a bell and a maid brought ice water," announced Flossie. "We had lots of fun."

"You must have!" chuckled Mr. Wardell. "But, Mr. Bobbsey," he went on, "it won't put us out a bit to have you all stay here. This is a big house and we have plenty of beds. It used to be a summer boarding house before I took it. We have plenty of food and there is no sense in your trying to go on in this storm."

"It is very kind of you to keep us over night," said Mrs. Bobbsey. "But are you sure it won't bother you?" she asked Mrs. Wardell.

"Not a bit of it!" was the hearty answer of the farmer's wife. "We are glad to have you.

It's a bit lonesome here for my children. They are always glad of company."

By the smiles on the faces and the gleams in the eyes of Lena and Charlie Mrs. Bobbsey could easily believe this to be true. So it was decided they would stay over night at the farmhouse and go on to Spruce Lake in the morning, if the storm had stopped by that time.

"I am in no special hurry," said Mr. Bobbsey. "We shall probably stay a month at the lake. But I do want to find Jake Doxey."

"You'll surely find him at the upper end of Spruce Lake," said Mr. Wardell. "Jake is a queer sort of man. He likes to be off by himself in the woods, hunting or fishing."

"Is there good fishing in Spruce Lake?" asked Bert of the farm boy.

"There certainly is," was the answer. "I caught some big ones when we went up there on an excursion earlier this summer. Have you a rod?"

"A fine one," said Bert. "I'd like to show it to you if I could get out to the barn. It's in our car."

"And I'll show you my fire engine that

pumps real water," said Freddie. "Mother, may I go and get my engine?" he asked.

At first Mrs. Bobbsey was going to say this could not be done. But she knew the children wanted a little amusement and it might be a kindness to Charlie and Lena to see something new, for they lived in a lonely part of the country.

So the Bobbsey twins, together with the two farm children, put the blankets over their heads again and dashed out to the barn through the night that was fast coming on. It was darker than usual because of the heavy clouds.

Meanwhile Mrs. Wardell and Mrs. Bobbsey went upstairs to arrange about beds for the night and Mr. Bobbsey and the farmer talked about lumber and where might be a good place to begin looking for the lost owner of the timber tract.

After Bert had displayed his rod and Nan her tennis racquet, in which, however, the Wardell children took only a polite interest as they did not play tennis, Lena and Charlie helped Bert, Nan, Flossie, and Freddie carry back to the farmhouse some of the playthings

the children had brought from Lakeport with
them, and there was soon a merry party of
youngsters having fun while the rain still came
down outside. The wind did not blow so hard
now, and there was only a clap of thunder
now and then—faint and far off as if the storm
was going away.

Freddie's fire engine was a marvel to Lena
and Charlie who had never seen anything like
it, and when it was taken out in the wood-
shed that opened from the kitchen, Freddie
was allowed to fill the tank with water, start
the pump, and send a stream across the shed,
where it did no harm.

Bert and Charlie looked again at the fishing pole and reel and Charlie told his new
friend some of the best spots around Spruce
Lake to catch fish.

Nan, Flossie, and Lena went upstairs where
the farm girl showed the visitors her room and
some of her "treasures," things like birds'
nests, queer stones and a collection of insects
that she had gathered in the woods and fields.

The odor of cooking soon filled the house,
and Freddie, for a wonder getting tired of
playing with his engine, cried·

"Gosh, I'm hungry!"

"It will soon be time to eat," said Charlie, with a smile.

"I'm glad we have company for supper, aren't you, Charlie?" his sister asked him as they went into the big dining room where a table was so filled with good things that, as Nan said, "it looked just like Thanksgiving."

"Yes, I'm glad it stormed so they have to stay," whispered Charlie to Lena. "We always have enough to eat but Ma has put out a lot of special stuff for the company."

Even with such appetites as healthy children always have there was no room for complaint after that meal. Freddie ate until, as Flossie said, he had to push back his chair a little from the edge of the table as he "was all swelling up."

The rain settled into a steady drizzle for the night and Mr. Bobbsey was glad he had stopped over as he felt sure he never could have driven the auto along the detour in the storm.

"I'm not sure we can even go along to-morrow," he said to his wife when they were all getting ready to go upstairs to bed.

"To-morrow, even if it rains, I can show you

another road to take," said Mr. Wardell. "It's a good bit longer, but it's a hard highway and will bring you to the lake all right."

"You said something about Flat Rock," said Mr. Bobbsey.

"That's the name of the camp to which you are going. There are several bungalows and cottages there, and a sort of hotel, or rather, central dining room. But I think that is closed. It's open only in July and August, I believe. You'll like it at Flat Rock Camp."

"No, the place is open. I telephoned from Crescent Falls," said Mr. Bobbsey.

"Why do they call it Flat Rock Camp?" asked Bert.

"Because," the farmer answered, "at that part of the lake is a big, flat rock out in the water near a sandy bathing beach."

"Oh, I'm going in bathing!" cried Freddie.

"So am I!" echoed Flossie.

"I expect they'll be in the water a great deal of the time," said Mrs. Wardell, with a smile. "It's natural for children."

"I fell in once," announced Freddie, as if it were something of which to be proud.

The night passed quietly enough. There were

no elevators for Freddie to ride up and down in and no electric buttons for Flossie to push to summon the maid with ice water.

The sun was shining when the Bobbsey twins awakened in the morning, though the detour road was rather deep in mud and pools of water.

"But you have to go along that for a short distance only," the farmer explained to Mr. Bobbsey. "Then you can swing on to a state highway that will bring you right to the lake."

"I'll try it," said the lumberman.

The children played together a little after breakfast, Charlie and Lena taking their visitors about the farm buildings and showing them the horses, cows, pigs, chickens, and ducks.

Meanwhile, Mr. Bobbsey looked over the auto to make sure it was in good order. Freddie's engine and Bert's fishing rod were put back in place, together with the sleeping garments the visitors had used over night, Nan saw to the careful disposal of her tennis racquet, and they were soon ready to travel on again.

They thanked the Wardells for their kindness and promised to stop and see them again some day, Mr. Bobbsey got as many directions as he could about looking for Jake Doxey, and at last they started off once more.

The going was not easy along the detour road, which was deep with mud, but in a short time they came out on a hard highway and made up for lost time. They expected to reach Spruce Lake about noon.

It was just past eleven o'clock when, in turning out of a patch of woods into a road that led through the open country, Nan gave an excited cry.

"What's the matter?" asked Bert, who was sitting near her.

"Did you see that boy?" asked Nan.

"What boy?" Bert inquired.

"That one we just passed in the woods." and Nan looked out of the side of the car and behind her. "Do you know who he was?"

"I saw some boy walking along under the trees," said Bert; "but I don't know who he was."

"He was Frank Denton!" exclaimed Nan.

"What! The boy from the junk wagon?"

"That's who he was," Nan said. "I saw him

as plainly as anything. Didn't you, Mother?"
she asked.

"No, Nan, I didn't," Mrs. Bobbsey replied.
"I don't believe you can be right, either. That
boy surely wouldn't be up here, so far away
from home, after the storm of last night. You
must have seen some one who looked like
him."

"No, Mother, I'm sure it was the same boy
that rolled out of the bundle of papers in the
junk wagon," said Nan. "I'm sure it was Frank
Denton." Nan stuck to this, though no one
would believe her. Even Bert said it couldn't
be so.

Some time later, through the trees along the
road, they caught sight of something gleaming
like silver in the sun.

"Look!" cried Flossie, pointing.

"That's Spruce Lake," her father said, and
a little later they came to an open place and
could see the pretty blue lake stretched out
below them, for they were up on a hill.

The road swung around a curve and in a
short time the auto was approaching a group
of log bungalows. Just beyond it could be seen
a great, flat-topped stone running down into

the water and there was a golden, sandy beach near it.

"Here we are," said Mr. Bobbsey, as he slowed up the car. "This is Flat Rock Camp. Here's where we stay."

The children began to murmur with delight. Freddie delved in among the valises eagerly.

"What are you after?" his mother asked.

"My fire engine."

"Oh, for mercy's sake wait until we unpack!" exclaimed Nan, with a laugh. "You ought to take that engine to bed with you!"

A man came from the large log building which Mrs. Bobbsey said must be the camp dining room. Around it were a number of log bungalows near which could be seen men, women and children.

"Is this Mr. Bobbsey and his family?" asked the man.

"Yes," was the answer. "I guess I talked to you over the telephone from Crescent Falls about getting a place here. Are you Mr. Truston?"

"That's my name. My wife will be out in a minute to take your wife to your bungalow and help you get settled. You brought some good weather with you," he added, with a laugh.

"Yes, and we left quite a storm behind us," replied Mr. Bobbsey.

The children were looking about them. Spruce Lake with the camp near the flat rock, the sparkling water, and the green trees made up what they thought was the most delightful place they had ever seen.

A woman came out of the big log dining room.

"There's my wife," explained Mr. Truston. "She——"

But he could say no more for the woman, with a sudden scream, began running toward the auto party while she shouted:

"He's after me again! Oh, take him away!"

CHAPTER XI

FREDDIE'S SPLASH

BERT BOBBSEY saw an animal darting from the dining cabin after Mrs. Truston, who was now running toward her husband near the auto.

"Oh, look!" cried Freddie, pointing to the animal which he and the others had seen almost as soon as Bert had. "It's a bear!"

"It's a wolf!" said Flossie. "He shan't get my Goldie!" she added, as she ran to be near her mother.

Mr. and Mrs. Bobbsey felt a little alarmed at first when they heard Mrs. Truston's screams and saw the animal chasing her. But as they looked at Mr. Truston and saw him laughing they knew it must be all right and that there was no danger. Mrs. Truston saw her husband laughing, and she did not seem to like it for she said:

"Jim, you horrid man, call Tamarack off! You know I can't bear him! Make him stop!"

Then the camp master shouted:

"Here, Tamarack! Come here!" He whistled and the animal, which was about as large as a very big cat and was mixed gray and black in color, turned aside and came toward Mr. Truston, who stood near the Bobbseys as they had alighted from their auto.

"Thank goodness!" murmured Mrs. Truston, when she saw her husband stoop down and pick up the animal. "I'd have fainted if he got at me again. I've had enough of him."

"Was that little bear going to eat you?" asked Freddie eagerly.

"'Tisn't a bear, it's a wolf," said Flossie.

"No, child, he wouldn't eat me, nor even hurt me," said Mrs. Truston. "And it is neither a bear nor a wolf. It's my husband's pet raccoon and he wants to tickle my feet every chance he gets. I keep him shut up when I'm around, but he got out and he made a dive for my ankles. He knows I can't bear to be tickled there and he is always trying it. Hold him tight now, Sam," she warned her husband. "If he gets loose I won't be able to attend to these new folks."

"All right!" chuckled the camp master, with a wink at Mr. Bobbsey.

"Oh, it's a raccoon!" exclaimed Bert, for now they all had a good look at the animal which was nestled quietly in Mr. Truston's arms.

"Isn't he cute!" murmured Nan.

"Will he bite?" asked Freddie, who waited to go nearer for a view until he was sure of this.

"He's as gentle as a kitten," explained the camp master. "But he has a funny habit of chasing after my wife and tickling her ankles. He has paws almost like hands, you see," and he held up one of the raccoon's legs to show the children. "It's funny when he chases my wife," he added.

"Funny!" exclaimed Mrs. Truston. "Well, I must say, Sam Truston, you have a queer idea of what's funny! I'd like to know how you'd like to be clawed by a 'coon!"

"He doesn't claw you, he just tickles you."

"Well, I don't like it and I wish you'd keep him shut up."

"All right, I will. I've had this pet a long time," went on Mr. Truston. "He's gentle and playful and my wife is the only one he chases. I guess he only does that because he knows she doesn't like him and he likes to hear her scream."

"Could I touch him?" asked Freddie.

"Sure! Play with him all you like," said Mr. Truston, and as his wife started back for the group of camp buildings with Mrs. Bobbsey, to show her the quarters the family were to have during their stay at Spruce Lake, there was no danger in putting down Tamarack, which was the name of the raccoon, or " 'coon," as Truston called him.

The animal soon made friends with the Bobbsey twins and they found, just as Mr. Truston had said, that he was as gentle and playful as their dog Snap or the old cat Snoop.

"Oh, isn't he lovely!" exclaimed Nan, as she cuddled Tamarack in her arms. Then Freddie and Flossie must have a turn at holding him and with each one the raccoon made himself perfectly at home.

Meanwhile Mr. Bobbsey and Mr. Truston were talking over camp matters and Mr. Bobb-

sey was told where he could leave his auto
under a shed. The Bobbsey bungalow was also
pointed out and Mr. Truston called for a man
to come and help move the baggage in. By this
time Mrs. Bobbsey had found out all she
needed to know from Mrs. Truston about the
times for meals and the family was soon getting
settled in its new vacation home.

Bert heard his father asking Mr. Truston
something about Jake Doxey and the camp
master said:

"I don't know the man. But if you know
he is up around the far end of the lake it ought
to be easy enough to find him. We have motorboats here and you can take one and voyage
up there."

"Oh, have you motorboats?" asked Bert
eagerly

"Yes, we have several. Moreover, one rowboat goes with your bungalow to use whenever
you like."

"Gee, what fun we'll have!" cried Bert to
Nan.

Bert and Nan both knew a little about running a motorboat and both could row.

They found that their bungalow was a very

pleasant one, with plenty of room for all of them. From the front porch a good view could be had of the lake. Behind the bungalow stretched the dark, green forest. It was part of this forest that Mr. Bobbsey wanted to buy from Jake Doxey to cut down the trees for lumber.

However, the children were more interested in Tamarack, the pet raccoon, in motorboats, and in the fun they would have on the lake and in the woods than they were in finding Jake Doxey.

Soon after the baggage had been put in the bungalow and Mr. and Mrs. Bobbsey were deciding on which rooms to give the children, Bert, Nan, and the smaller twins, after playing with Tamarack, saw coming toward their bungalow two other girls and two boys. One girl and boy were about the ages of Nan and Bert while the others were about like Flossie and Freddie.

"Are you the Bobbsey twins?" asked the older boy, nodding at Bert.

"Yes," was the answer. "How did you know about us?"

"Oh, Mr. Truston—he's the camp master,

you know—told us you were coming," answered the new boy. "And we're glad of it, because a lot of the fellows and girls who were camping here earlier in the summer have gone home. My name is Ned Floyd, and this is my sister Mary. And these others," he pointed to the smaller children, "are Jerry and Susan Bickart. We've all been coming here to camp a long time and we like it."

"It's a dandy place," said Bert, and then he told the names of his sister and brother. Soon all eight children had made friends and were talking and laughing as if they had known one another a long time. Bert spoke of the raccoon.

"Oh, yes," said Ned, "he always chases Mrs. Truston, because, I guess, he knows she'll run away from him. But he never hurts anybody."

"If he chases me I'll run," said Flossie.

"If he chases me I'll squirt water on him from my fire engine," threatened Freddie.

"Oh, have you got a fire engine?" asked Jerry eagerly. Then he and Freddie and Flossie and Susan went to get the wonderful toy, Susan running back to her bungalow to get her doll, for Flossie had hers.

Meanwhile Bert and Nan, Ned and Mary, were talking over plans for having fun, boating, swimming, tennis, and fishing. The older Bobbsey twins were glad to find these new friends.

After a while, as the four sat talking near the bungalow where the Bobbsey family was to stay, they heard shouts and laughter from the edge of the lake.

"That's Freddie squirting his fire engine," explained Bert.

"Has he really an engine that pumps?" asked Ned. "Let's go and take a look at it."

"Sure," agreed Bert. "It works with a spring motor pump. Anyhow, we'd better see what Flossie and Freddie are doing," he added.

As the four neared the lake they could see, through the trees, that the smaller twins and their new playmates had stopped playing with the fire engine and were gathered about a swing that was fastened to the outstretched limb of a big tree.

"That swing is pretty near the water, isn't it?" asked Bert.

"It goes right out over the water if you swing far enough," stated Ned.

Just then it was Freddie's turn to swing, and Bert and Nan saw Jerry and Susan give him a big push which sent him on a long swaying journey. Out and out went the swing with the little boy on the board.

"Oh, he's going right out over the water!" exclaimed Nan.

"There's no danger," said Ned. "We do it all the while."

But there was danger for Freddie. A moment later, as the swing was out over the lake, on the edge of which the tree stood, the little boy slipped off the seat and fell in with a great splash.

"Oh! Oh!" cried Nan. "Oh!"

"Come on!" yelled Bert, dashing toward the lake followed by Ned.

CHAPTER XII

BERT'S JUMPING FISH

"FREDDIE'S in the water! Freddie's in the water!" cried Jerry and Susan as they saw what had happened to their new playmate on his first play at the swing. "Freddie's in the water!"

"Oh, get him out! Get him out!" yelled Flossie. She was glad she had not gone in the swing with her brother as she had first wanted to do. Freddie had said he wanted to go alone and "swing high." Yes, indeed, Flossie was glad she hadn't sat in with him only to fall out in the water. "Freddie is going to be drowned!" Flossie was beginning to cry now.

But by this time Bert and Ned, followed more slowly by Nan and Mary, were at the edge of the lake, and Bert, who had already taken off his coat and kicked off his loose shoes, shouted:

"I'll save you, Freddie! I'll save you!"

The little fellow, who had gone down under water, now bobbed up again and began splashing about. So he probably did not hear Bert's cry of rescue, for his ears were filled with water.

But Freddie knew how to swim a little and his father had often told him what to do if he fell in. Freddie was now trying to do it.

However, Bert made a clean dive into the water from a ledge, near where the big swing tree grew, and was soon striking out to get his small brother.

"I'll help!" yelled Ned and he, too, made a dive in after taking off his coat and shoes as Bert had done.

For a moment Nan had been much frightened, but when Mary called out that the water wasn't very deep, and when Nan saw her twin brother and Ned splashing their way toward where Freddie was struggling, she felt sure he would be saved.

He was. The older boys soon pulled him over to shore where the water was so shallow they could all stand up, and after Freddie got over a little choking, caused by some water he had swallowed and by some getting up his nose, he was all right.

"What did you want to do that for?" asked Bert, as he helped his brother up the bank and began to shake some of the water off.

"What did I do?" Freddie asked.

"You jumped out of the swing, didn't you?"

"No," said the little boy, "I—now—I—I fell out. I slipped. I couldn't help it."

"You shouldn't have swung so high," declared Nan.

"Well, maybe I shouldn't," admitted Freddie. "But they gave me an awful hard push," and he nodded toward Jerry, Susan and Flossie.

"He told us to push him high—away up to the sky," said Flossie, drying her tears, now that she saw her brother was safe. "Only he didn't go up to the sky. He fell into the water."

"I should say he did!" chuckled Bert. "But you'd better not do it again," he added.

"Oh, I won't!" Freddie promised.

"It wasn't your fault," went on Bert to the smaller children, for he noticed that Jerry and Susan looked rather frightened over what had happened. "Freddie shouldn't have told you to swing him so high. It was his own fault."

"I won't do it again," Freddie promised again. "I'll only swing a little bit."

"So will I," added Flossie.

After all no great harm was done, and as the boys had on old play suits the wetting did no damage. It was so warm that the dive into the lake felt good, so, after letting the water drip off them, they sat down on a warm rock in the sun to dry out.

Mr. and Mrs. Bobbsey, having settled about the bungalow and the dining room, came over to see what the children were doing, and of course they heard what had happened. Mr. Bobbsey gave Freddie strict orders never to swing out over the water again and the little fellow promised to obey.

After the Bobbsey twins had been shown about the camp by their four new friends, it was time to eat. Quite a party of children, with their fathers and mothers, gathered in the big log dining room and had a fine meal. The news of what had happened to Freddie passed around and all the campers looked at him. But this did not bother Freddie.

"I'm going to be a fireman," he said; "and firemans aren't ever afraid of water. Not even when they fall in."

"It's a good thing your name is Bobbsey," chuckled Mr. Truston, who was seeing that the waiters served every one in the dining cabin. "Yes, indeed, a good thing you are named Bobbsey."

"Why?" asked Freddie.

"Because you bobbed up so nicely after you fell into the water," said the camp master, with a laugh.

Many others joined in, but Freddie did not mind this little joke about him. He went right on eating and said:

"I'm a fireman and firemans aren't afraid of water."

This was not the first time the Bobbsey twins had been at a forest camp, and though the beds in the bungalow were a little different from those at home in Lakeport, the four were soon sound asleep after the day of adventures.

"What'll we do to-day?" asked Bert of Ned as the two boys met after breakfast. Nan and Mary had decided to play a game of tennis if the grown-up folk did not use the court and

were on the way to "Pickerel Cove," as Ned called it, a place where, so he said, there were always fish to be caught.

"Gee, this is great!" murmured Bert, as they took their places on a shady bank and cast in their baited hooks. "I'm glad we came up here."

" 'Tis a nice place," agreed Ned. Both boys talked in low voices so as not to scare the fish. They believed the fish could hear and might keep away if they made too much noise.

For a little while nothing happened. The cork bobs of the boys' lines floated on the surface of the pool, and, now and then, a small dragon fly would alight on the cord and flicker its four gauzy wings. In the trees and bushes birds sang and bees hummed. The sun was shining warmly and there was a sweet, spicy odor of woods.

Suddenly Ned's cork float went under and he gave his pole a jerk and began winding his line up on the reel.

"You've got one!" whispered Bert, wishing he had had such good luck.

"Yes, and he's a big one by the way he pulls," said the other boy. "Golly! A big one!"

The fish was now cutting back and forth in the water, trying to get off the hook, but Ned reeled in and landed a good-sized perch.

"I wish I could catch one!" murmured Bert.

Hardly had he spoken when he felt a jerk on his line. He began to pull in, forgetting about winding the line on his reel. And then, feeling the pull stronger, Bert suddenly yanked up on his pole as he had been used to doing before he had a reel.

Something green and glistening with water drops flew up from the pool and sailed over Bert's head, landing on the grass back of him.

"What kind of a fish have I caught?" Bert yelled.

A moment later there sounded a shrill, excited cry back of him which he knew was Freddie's voice. Freddie yelled:

"Bert! Bert! You've caught a jumping fish! Oh, look!"

CHAPTER XIII

A QUEER FIREMAN

BERT and Ned looked at each other in surprise. Then Bert, with a murmur of wonder, scrambled to his feet and started back toward the high grass where he knew he had landed his "jumping fish." He was wondering how Freddie came to be so near, for when Bert and Ned had gone fishing Freddie was playing with his fire engine in company with Jerry, his new chum.

"Look at the jumping fish, Bert!" exclaimed Freddie, as his brother ran toward him. The small boy pointed to a clump of tall grass in which something was moving about very fast.

"Jumping fish!" said Bert. "All fish jump when you pull them out of the water."

"They don't jump like this one," argued Freddie.

Bert knew he had caught something different. He had been sure of that when he had seen the glistening green thing fly over his head.

Not stopping to ask Freddie how he happened to be there, but rightly guessing that the little fellow had wandered over to see what luck the young fishermen had, Bert made a dart for the clump of grass. By this time Ned was at his side.

"Something is jumping around mighty lively!" exclaimed Ned.

"More lively than any fish I ever saw," agreed Bert. "And did you see how green it looked when I yanked it over my head?"

"I sure did! First time I knew there were any green fish in Spruce Lake."

"Don't let him get away!" shouted Freddie, for whatever was on the end of Bert's line was skipping this way and that in the grass and seemed likely to pull loose from the hook.

Then the jumping creature gave an unusually big leap and showed itself above the grass. It could be plainly seen in the bright sun, and Bert yelled:

"It's a frog!"

"And a whopping big one, too!" added Ned, when he saw the animal.

"Oh, how did you catch a frog?" Freddie wanted to know, for he, also, now saw distinctly the jumping creature.

"He must have got on my hook by mistake," observed Bert. "Whoa, now!" he added, as he found his line and began pulling it in to get hold of the frog. The jumper was frightened and tried to get away, but the hook was caught near its mouth and held firmly.

"Can I have him?" asked Freddie. "I mean after you get him off the hook."

"What do you want of a jumping frog?" asked Ned, with a laugh.

"Maybe I can get another and train 'em and hitch 'em to my fire engine to pull it," Freddie answered.

"You can't train a frog," Bert declared. "Not this one—he's too wild. Whoa! Stand still!" he cried. "I won't hurt you!"

The frog, now that he felt himself being pulled by the line and hook, jumped about more wildly than ever. But Bert soon had him in his hands and, very gently, took the hook out of the animal's lip. It had only gone through one edge and had not been swallowed.

"There you are," Bert said, as he loosed the

frog from the sharp point. "You are hurt hardly at all."

"A frog has tough skin," Ned said. "It doesn't hurt to stick a hook in it."

"Oh, let me have the frog!" begged Freddie. "I'll tame him and have him for a pet."

Bert had a notion to do as his little brother asked, but Mr. Frog had his own ideas on being kept even a pet prisoner. He was wet and slippery, was that big, green frog. He was the largest one the boys had ever seen. And suddenly giving a squirm, he got out of Bert's grasp, fell to the ground, and at once began to jump fast and far toward the water.

"There he goes!" cried Ned.

"Catch him!" shouted Bert.

"I'll get him!" Freddie said.

Though all three boys ran after the frog, he was such a big one and such a fast and broad jumper that he easily got away from them.

Right to the edge of the bank Bert, Freddie, and Ned raced after the green fellow, but when he reached the jumping-off place that frog just gave one, big jump and into the water he went ker-plop!

"Gosh, what a splash he made!" Freddie exclaimed.

"Almost as big a splash as you made when you fell off the swing," said Ned.

"Well, he's gone, and I'm just as glad," remarked Bert. "He's had trouble enough. Now maybe I'll catch a fish."

"How did he get on your hook?" asked Freddie.

"Oh, he just nibbled at my bait as a fish would," Bert answered. "And when I yanked up, instead of reeling in as I should have done, I pulled the hook into the side of his mouth and then sailed him up through the air over my head."

The excitement was now ended and Bert and Ned sat down again to keep on with their fishing. Freddie wished he had brought along a pole and line when he decided to follow his brother and Ned to see where they were going. However, Ned had an extra cord in his pocket and some spare hooks, so he fixed up a little fishing outfit for Freddie, who was greatly delighted when he was allowed to cast in beside his brother.

Bert's wish that he might catch a fish soon came to pass, for he hauled out a larger perch than Ned had caught. Then Ned had another bit of luck and after a while the two older boys had caught quite a string of large-sized ones.

"I wish I could catch one," Freddie said, after having pulled his hook up several times, only to find the bait nibbled off.

"You don't pull quickly enough when you feel a nibble," Bert told him. "You have to be quick to catch fish."

A little later, to his delight, Freddie pulled in a large sunfish which, Ned said, was almost as good as a perch.

"Now I'm a fisherman and a fireman," said Freddie gleefully.

The boys fished a while longer, catching so many that when they got back to the camp Mr. Truston said:

"You have a fine mess there. I'll have the cook clean 'em and fry 'em for supper."

The Bobbsey and the Floyd families had fried fish for dinner that night, and very good they were, too. The boys, including Freddie who had succeeded in catching a second big sunfish, were quite pleased at having thus helped provide the meal.

Next morning, when Bert and Ned were planning to get a rowboat and visit Umbrella Island and some of the other islands in the lake, Mrs. Bobbsey heard Flossie crying at the back of the bungalow.

"Has anything happened, my dear?" she called to the little girl.

"Oh, I've lost my doll!" was the answer. "I've lost Goldie."

"How did it happen?" asked Mrs. Bobbsey, going out to her little daughter.

"I was walking along through the woods," Flossie said, "and I was carrying Goldie under my arm. I saw some red berries and when I went to pick them I laid Goldie down and when I went back to get her I couldn't find her."

"I guess you forgot where you put her," said Bert, who was about to start off with Ned. "Come and show me where you think you left your doll, Flossie, and Ned and I will hunt for her."

"Maybe a wolf carried her off," sobbed the little girl.

"There aren't any wolves in these woods," Ned declared.

"The boys will find Goldie for you," said Mrs. Bobbsey. "Go along with them, Flossie, to show them where you picked the berries. And you'll bring her back here, won't you, Bert?" she asked.

"Oh, yes; Mother, sure," he promised. "Ned and I are going to Umbrella Island."

"Be careful," his mother warned him.

Flossie led her brother and Ned back through the woods the way she had come after picking some red berries and she showed where she thought she had laid her doll under a tree.

There was no sign of Goldie. However, Bert and his camp chum had sharp eyes, so, thinking Flossie might have made a mistake in pointing out the tree where she thought she had left her doll, they looked about under others and pretty soon they found the missing Goldie beneath a tree near a big rock, sleeping peacefully on a bed of green moss.

"Oh, now I 'member; I left her here!" cried Flossie, in delight. "I 'member about the big rock! At first I forgot."

"Well, now you're all right," said Ned, and he and Bert turned to take Flossie back to camp before going off on a trip of their own. As they neared the Bobbsey bungalow and turned the corner they saw something on the porch that caused them much wonder and delight.

Freddie had left his toy fire engine, with the tank filled and the spring pump wound up, near the front steps. Just as Bert and the others came within sight of it Flossie shouted:

'What a funny fireman!"

"Well, what do you know about that?" cried Ned.

"Somebody must have trained him!" declared Bert. "Hey, Freddie! Look at the queer fireman!" he called to his small brother, who was coming along the woodland path, having been on a little trip by himself.

CHAPTER XIV

THE WOODLAND PICNIC

WITH shouts of surprise, Bert, Ned and Flossie hurried on to the bungalow on the porch of which Freddie had left his fire engine. As the other children drew near, Freddie himself came running around the corner.

"What's the matter?" he asked, hearing the shouts.

"Look at your fire engine!" called Flossie, laughing as she pointed.

"Is it busted?" Freddie quickly asked.

But nothing like that had happened. And when Freddie looked and saw what had happened he had to laugh with the others.

Tamarack, the tame raccoon, had found the engine, had taken the hose in his hand-like paws, and, in some manner, must have turned on the pump, for a spray of water was coming from the length of rubber hose and Tamarack in delight was turning it now on himself and now against the side of the bungalow or on the porch floor.

"What a funny fireman!" cried Freddie, capering about.

"He's awfully cute," said Flossie.

"You'd think he was trained," added Bert.

"He sure loves water," chuckled Ned. "But I've heard Mr. Truston say all 'coons do. Look at him squirt, would you?"

Tamarack held the hose so the little stream of water went right in his mouth which he seemed to open as if he were laughing. It made the children laugh so hard to see him that Mrs. Bobbsey came out to see what the matter was and Mrs. Truston, hearing the shouts, started from her bungalow near by.

"What is it?" asked Mrs. Bobbsey, not at first seeing the animal.

"Oh, Tamarack found Freddie's engine," stated Bert, "and he's making believe put out a fire."

"Did you ever see anything so clever?" asked Mrs. Bobbsey of the camp master's wife.

"Oh, that 'coon!" exclaimed Mrs. Truston, when she caught a glimpse of Tamarack.

"He's too smart! Though I never saw him do anything like that before. But he's very fond of water. He takes a bath almost every day and every bit of food he gets he takes down and dips in the lake before he eats it. The only thing he doesn't wash before eating is green corn."

Whether Tamarack knew Mrs. Truston's voice or saw her, was not made clear, but, all of a sudden, the raccoon dropped the fire-engine hose and made a dash for the camp master's wife.

"Oh, don't let him tickle my ankles!" she cried, and with a scream she started to run back to her bungalow. "Keep him back!"

However, Tamarack did not intend to chase her. He made a playful dash, as a dog sometimes does, and, having seen Mrs. Truston hurry away, he went back on the porch. It almost seemed as if he were laughing to himself.

"He just loves my fire engine," said Freddie, as the smart little animal again picked up the hose.

By this time the tank was empty and no more water was spurting out of the hose, and

as water was what Tamarack best liked he
had no further use for the toy, but came walking toward the children.

"I guess he's hungry," said Flossie.

"I'll get him an apple," offered Freddie, for
he had seen Mr. Truston feed the pet this
fruit. "And then," went on the little fellow,
"I'm going to make him squirt my hose some
more. Maybe," he went on with a sudden, new
thought, "I could get up a show, have Tamarack in it and make some money."

"Maybe," chuckled Bert.

"Mrs. Truston wouldn't come to your
show," said Ned. "She would be afraid of being tickled."

However, the raccoon seemed satisfied to
stay on the Bobbsey porch as long as Freddie
fed him pieces of apple and Mrs. Truston's
ankles were in no danger of being tickled. Bert
and Ned left Freddie to play as long as he
liked with the raccoon and the engine, the older
boys going off in a boat to Umbrella Island
where they caught some fish. On the way back
the boys rowed past another island.

"What's the name of that one?" Bert asked
his chum.

"Forest Island. It has more trees on it than any other and we have lots of fun there."

"What sort of fun?" asked Bert.

"Picnic fun. That's the place where everybody from this camp goes whenever there's a picnic."

"When is there going to be another picnic?" Bert wanted to know.

"Anybody can get up one whenever he likes," was Ned's reply. "Our folks had one about a week ago."

"Then, I'm going to ask my mother to get up a picnic for Forest Island!" exclaimed Bert. "Will you and your sister come?"

"Sure, we will. So will anybody you ask. It's lots of fun to go on picnics."

Bert began to row faster to get back to the mainland more quickly so he might propose the picnic to his mother, and he and Ned soon had the boat at the Floyd dock.

"We're going to have our boat to-morrow," said Bert, as he got out with his fish. "I heard my father talking to Mr. Truston about it."

"You can use ours as much as you want to," replied Ned, for it was in his father's boat that the boys had gone to Umbrella Island.

"Picnic!" exclaimed Mrs. Bobbsey, when Bert spoke to her about it. "Why, of course we can get up a picnic."

"Hurray!" cried Bert. "We'll go to Forest Island and have fun! Ned and I will catch fish and we'll cook 'em over a campfire."

"May I invite Mary?" asked Nan.

"Yes," her mother said.

"And I'll ask Jerry!" chimed in Freddie.

"I'll ask Susan," said Flossie.

"Yes, ask all your little friends," said Mrs. Bobbsey, and from then on for the next few days nothing was talked of but the picnic to be held on Forest Island.

Those were happy days at Spruce Lake. The Bobbsey twins thought they had never had such fun. But then they said that about every place they went, so you couldn't go much by it. It certainly was lovely, though, in the woods around the lake. They went in swimming, rowed about the lake, walked in the woods, and Nan met some girls who played tennis with her when they could get the single tennis court the camp afforded.

Mr. Bobbsey was somewhat disappointed

that he could not find Jake Doxey to buy the timberland from him. Several men about the camp reported having seen the missing man in several places, but each time Mr. Bobbsey went there Jake Doxey was gone.

"He's a hard person to find," said Mr. Bobbsey.

But Bert, Nan, and the others were too much interested in getting ready for the picnic to think much about Jake Doxey. Several of the families living near the Bobbsey bungalow planned to go on the picnic, and at last the great day came.

Lunches had been packed in boxes and baskets, Bert and Ned had their fishing rods, and it was nearly all Mrs. Bobbsey could do to prevent Freddie from taking his fire engine. But she told him he could not use it if he did take it so he left it in the bungalow.

Mr. and Mrs. Truston were to go on the picnic, and several of the fathers and mothers would go with their children. But as Mr. Bobbsey was waiting to get word from a man who felt sure he knew where Jake Doxey was, the father of the four twins decided he would not go to Forest Island.

Of course this was a disappointment to the children, for they loved to have their father with them, but it could not be helped.

"Have a good time and don't get lost!" called Mr. Bobbsey to his family as they started off in a rowboat, one of several that was to take the picnic party to Forest Island. It was a bright, sunny day.

The Bobbsey boat was the first to reach the place. Bert and Nan rowed it well and the island was not far from the main shore. Freddie was the first to jump out as the bow of the boat ran up on a sandy beach. He was quickly followed by Flossie.

The smaller twins were running up toward the cool, green woods when, all of a sudden, as Bert and Nan were helping their mother take out the baskets and boxes of lunch, Freddie stopped and called:

"Did you hear that?"

"Hear what?" asked Bert.

"That funny noise," replied the smaller Bobbsey boy.

"I heard it, too," whispered Flossie, walking back toward her mother. "It sounded like —now—like a lion roaring."

"Maybe it was a tiger," said Freddie in a low voice.

"Nonsense!" laughed Mrs. Bobbsey. "Don't be silly!"

"But there is a queer noise," said Nan, as she looked across the lake at the other boats now drawing near. "Don't you hear something, Bert? Listen!"

CHAPTER XV

LOST ON FOREST ISLAND

BERT BOBBSEY put his load of picnic lunch down on the sand and tilted his head toward the line of forest trees not far away. For a moment he heard nothing but the wind in the leaves, the lap of water on the pebbly and sandy shore, and the noise of the oars in the other boats that were drawing toward the beach.

Then, above these other sounds, Bert did hear something that was different. It echoed in the woods off to the left. At times it was loud and again he was hardly able to hear it.

"What is it?" asked Nan, in wonder.

"Do you hear it, Mother?" asked Bert.

Mrs. Bobbsey listened and said:

"Yes, I hear some sort of animal, I think."

"Maybe it's a wild animal!" exclaimed Freddie very much interested.

"Maybe it's an elephant," suggested Flossie eagerly.

"Don't be silly," advised Mrs. Bobbsey. "If it's any animal at all it is a cow."

"I hope it is a cow," said Bert. "Then we can have some fresh milk with our picnic lunch."

"First you have to catch the cow," said Nan, with a laugh, "and maybe that won't be easy."

"Maybe it's a wild cow," suggested Freddie. "They're terribly hard to catch if you haven't a lasso, and we haven't any."

"You're right there," Bert said, laughing. "And I'm not going to try to catch any wild island cow."

"Let's see if we can hear the noise again," suggested Nan.

So they listened and did, indeed, hear a confused sort of rumbling, grunting and squealing sound, or rather, several sounds. By this time a number of other boats had come to shore and when Ned Floyd got out of one and ran to where the Bobbsey family was standing, he asked:

"What's the matter?"

"We heard a noise," Flossie answered.

"Like a wild cow," added Freddie.

"I don't hear anything," said Ned, and, truly enough, the noise was no longer to be heard. "I guess it was the wind," he went on.

"No, it wasn't the wind," said Bert. "It was some animal, but I guess it may be a dog or a cow."

"It could be," Ned agreed. "Sometimes men come over here fishing and one might bring his dog and forget it. But I don't see why anybody would bring a cow here. There isn't much here for a cow to eat."

"That's very true," said Mrs. Bobbsey.

"Maybe a cow could swim over from the mainland," suggested Nan.

"Well, we'll take a look around after we all get ashore," said Ned, and Bert and he planned to make up a hunting party to see what had made the queer noise which was now no longer to be heard.

Soon all the boatloads of merry picnickers had been landed, and the children, including the Bobbsey twins, began racing about here and there, delighted to spend a day in the woods. The fathers and mothers, under the guidance of Mr. and Mrs. Truston who had brought many parties to Forest Island, took charge of the lunches and began to plan for dinner in a grove where there were rustic tables and benches.

Such fun as the picnickers had! Even the fathers and mothers played about under the trees. As for Flossie and Freddie and their little chums, Jerry and Susan, as Mrs. Truston said, "it's a wonder their legs don't drop off they run about so!"

Nan, Mary and some of the older girls wandered about, played ball for a time, visited a spring on the island where there were clumps of graceful green ferns, and ended by taking off their shoes and stockings and going wading in a shallow pool.

Some of the boys got up a baseball game, but Bert and Ned decided they must do something more serious, so they took their rods and went fishing over on the other side of the island. They had good luck, and they brought back several perch and two bass which Mr. Truston cleaned and fried in a pan over an open fire.

"It's like regular camping," said Bert, in delight.

"And there's nothing better to eat in camp than fish and bacon," declared Ned, as the appetizing smell of the cooking floated on the forest air.

"Did you hear any more queer noises, my dears?" asked Mrs. Bobbsey of Freddie and Flossie as, tired out with their running around, they came back to the grove when it was near the lunch hour.

"Oh, we forgot all about listening," Freddie said.

"We'll listen after we eat," promised Flossie. "Oh, I'm so thirsty! I could drink a quart of water!"

"I could drink two quarts!" boasted Freddie.

There was a jolly time at the lunch tables, several families dining together. The Floyds and Bickarts sat at the same table with the Bobbseys, and the twins and their camp chums talked and laughed so much one might have wondered how they found time to eat.

But they did, and at last there was nothing left of the lunches that had been brought to Forest Island. Then came more fun in the woods for the children, while the older folks sat under the trees and talked.

But all days must come to an end and this

happy one had to do the same. The sun began to go down, shadows began to lengthen, and at last Mr. Truston blew on the horn. This was the signal for all the children to come to the grove where the tables were set and get ready to go aboard the boats and start back for the camp on the mainland.

One after another the children drifted in, Bert, Nan, Ned, Mary, Jerry, and Susan. They were tired but happy, and declared that they never had had such a wonderful time.

"Where are Flossie and Freddie?" asked Mrs. Bobbsey when all the children but the two small twins had reported. "Did you see them, Bert?"

"I saw them a little while ago," he answered. "They were walking through the woods off that way," and he pointed toward a part of the island where the trees and bushes grew very thick.

"I hope they didn't go too far," said Mrs. Bobbsey.

"I told them not to, for I knew it was getting near time to go home," stated Bert. "I'll go and see if I can find them."

He and Ned, with some other boys, hastened

away, shouting and calling the names of Flossie and Freddie. But the missing twins did not answer. The sun sank down farther in the west. Mrs. Bobbsey began to get anxious.

Word soon spread around that Flossie and Freddie Bobbsey had wandered away and were lost, and then some of the fathers and mothers took up the search. Though they went off in different directions, no trace of Freddie and Flossie could be found.

"I guess they're lost," said Nan, with a sigh, as she came back from a search which she and Mary had started by themselves.

"Well, Forest Island isn't very big," said Mr. Truston. "We'll soon find them."

CHAPTER XVI

OUT IN THE GALE

WHEN Bert and Nan Bobbsey came back to the dining grove, after having gone some distance into the forest without finding the lost children, and when others came back with no news, Mrs. Bobbsey began to feel that she might have to stay on the island all night to find lost Flossie and Freddie.

It was getting later and darker, the wind was beginning to blow, and some of the mothers began to feel that they had better start for the mainland without waiting to find the lost ones. But no one wanted to go away and leave Mrs. Bobbsey in her trouble.

"I'm afraid a storm is coming up," said Mr. Truston when he and several men had not been able to find out where Flossie and Freddie had wandered.

"Let the other folks go home," suggested

Mrs. Bobbsey. "They should not stay on my account. I will remain here with Nan and Bert until I find Flossie and Freddie."

"Oh, no. We wouldn't leave you," said Mrs. Floyd.

"I could row over to the mainland and get Mr. Bobbsey and bring him back with me if you wanted me to," said Mr. Bickart.

"I don't believe my husband is in our bungalow," said Mrs. Bobbsey. "He started off early this morning in a motorboat to find Jake Doxey, and he hardly expected to be back before dark. Oh, I don't see where Flossie and Freddie can be!"

"We'd better get up another searching party," suggested Mr. Truston, "and go over the island foot by foot. We'll make up four parties, one going to the east, another to the south, one to the north and one to the west. We must shout and call. Surely they will hear us then."

It did not take long to make up four parties of the men, women and older girls and boys And while the smaller children were left in charge of Mrs. Truston, the others started off. Bert and Nan went with their mother toward the south, and they had not gone very far along a trail no one had taken before when Bert suddenly called:

"Hark!"

"What is it?" asked his mother nervously.

"I heard a noise," Bert said in a low voice. "It sounded like the little twins talking."

"I heard it, too," said Nan.

A moment later, as they came into a little open glade, they all heard Flossie's voice saying:

"Aren't they cute!"

"I wish we could take them home," said Freddie.

"Thank goodness, here they are!" exclaimed Mrs. Bobbsey with a sigh of relief. "Flossie! Freddie! Where are you? What are you doing?" she called.

"Here we are," announced Flossie, and from a little thicket of bushes across the glade out stepped Flossie.

"And we've found out what made that funny noise we heard when we first came here," added Freddie, walking out beside Flossie. "It was pigs."

"Pigs!" shouted Bert.

"A big pig. He was grunting," went on Flossie.

"And a lot of little pigs. They were squealing. That's what made the noise," added Freddie. "We found it and here they are. Come and see 'em!"

Hurrying across the glade, Mrs. Bobbsey and the older twins looked where Flossie and Freddie pointed. There, nestled in a bed of ferns, was a mother pig and six little ones. The old pig looked up at the Bobbseys, blinked her eyes sleepily and grunted. The little pigs snuggled up to their mother and made funny, squeaking noises.

"Aren't they nice?" asked Flossie. "We found 'em!"

"We're going to take 'em home for pets," added Freddie. "A 'coon is a nice pet but pigs are better. We'll take 'em in our boat."

"No, indeed you won't!" said Mrs. Bobbsey, ready to laugh now that the lost children were found.

"Oh, why not?" teased Freddie.

"They're awfully cute!" sighed Flossie.

"They look cute here," said Mrs. Bobbsey; "but they wouldn't be so cute grunting and digging around our bungalow. Besides, they must belong to some farmer around here and we can't take his pigs."

"I guess he doesn't want 'em or he wouldn't let 'em be over on this island all alone," stated Freddie.

"Maybe the old pig swam over here from the mainland and has been living here a long time," suggested Bert. "I guess that's how it was."

"And the little pigs swam over on her back," added Flossie. "I wish I had seen 'em. They must have looked cute."

"Well, as all the folks are looking for you two lost ones," said Mrs. Bobbsey, "we must get back and save them tramping about any more. Besides, it is getting late and there is going to be a storm."

This was evident. The wind was rising, clouds were covering the sky, and the distant rumble of thunder could be heard behind the hills.

"Why did you two wander away over here?" asked Bert of his small brother and sister as they started back for the dining grove.

"Oh, we wanted to find out what animals

made that funny noise," explained Freddie. "So we just walked along and pretty soon we heard the noise again and then we found the pigs."

"Didn't you think that you were lost and that we would be looking for you?" asked Nan.

"Oh, we weren't lost," said Flossie quickly. "We were with the pigs."

"We were just going to try to make 'em walk back with us when you came along," added Freddie.

"Didn't you hear us calling you?" asked Bert.

The little twins said they had not. They had been so interested in seeking the cause of the strange noises that they had paid little heed to anything else and had not realized how late it was getting.

Every one of the picnic party was glad the lost ones had been found. Mr. Truston blew the horn to call back all the searchers and the boats were soon being rowed back to the camp, all safe and sound after an hour of worry.

"I guess the pig and her family came from

the mainland," said the camp keeper when the children asked him about the animals. "Some farmer must have owned them, but he probably doesn't know where they are now. But I'll pass word around and maybe the owner will come after his animals."

"I wish he'd give me a little pig," murmured Flossie. "I love a little pig. They're so pink and they grunt so nicely."

"No pigs for me!" declared Nan. "I would rather have a raccoon."

"Yes, a 'coon is nice, too," admitted Flossie. "But I like pigs."

Though the rowers in the boats made their oars go fast, they hardly reached the camp before the storm broke and the rain came down in a burst of wind. There was not much thunder and lightning yet, but the wind was a regular gale, as Mr. Truston said.

The Bobbseys hurried to their bungalow, getting a little wet as they ran beneath the trees.

"Thank goodness, we are home safe!" exclaimed Mrs. Bobbsey.

"Daddy! Daddy!" cried Flossie, rushing into the bungalow. "We found some pigs!"

"Will you buy one for us?" added Freddie.

But Mr. Bobbsey did not answer. He was not in the bungalow, though his wife had thought to see him back after his trip up the lake in the motorboat to look for Jake Doxey.

A step sounded out on the porch and the children, thinking it was their father, ran to the door. But it was Mr. Tate, one of the men campers who had not gone to Forest Island.

"Mr. Bobbsey told me to tell you," said Mr. Tate, "that he might not be back until late as he had to go almost to the upper end of the lake to find the man he is looking for. I saw him start out in his motorboat. He came back after going up a way and gave me that message for you."

"Oh, thank you for telling us," said Mrs. Bobbsey. "I suppose he will be along soon now. He can't look for Jake Doxey after dark."

"I don't see how he can," replied Mr. Tate. "It's night now."

Indeed, it was quite dark and lights were soon aglow in the camp.

"We must eat supper," said Mrs. Bobbsey to Nan.

"Isn't Daddy going to be here to eat with

us?" asked Flossie, and her voice was fretful, for she was tired from racing about on Forest Island.

"He'll be along pretty soon," said Bert cheerfully.

"I wish he'd come now so I could tell him about the pigs," sighed Freddie.

But as they got ready to eat there was no sign of Mr. Bobbsey. It was not a very jolly meal. It grew darker and the wind howled around the bungalow. It was a regular "gale," as a sailor would say. Mrs. Bobbsey did not feel at all happy that her husband was out in the boat in all the storm. Spruce Lake could get very rough at times.

"Oh, when will Daddy come?" half sobbed Flossie.

CHAPTER XVII

BERT ON THE TRAIL

AFTER a while Flossie and Freddie Bobbsey forgot to worry about their father not coming home. They were so tired that, try as they did when supper was over to stay awake, they could not. First the head of Flossie would nod to one side. Then Freddie's head would bob over on the other side as the two tried to sit up in their chairs.

Then Freddie's eyes would close and next Flossie would shut hers. Sometimes the smaller twins managed to open one eye for a little while, but soon both closed again.

"You two must go to bed!" declared Mrs. Bobbsey.

"But we want to stay up until Daddy comes home!" pleaded the "little fireman."

"He will come when you are asleep," suggested Nan, with a look at her mother.

"Oh, then that's all right," answered Flossie drowsily. "But when he comes let him come to my room."

"And to mine, too," begged Freddie. "I want to tell him how we got lost."

"And how we found the pigs," added Flossie.

"Yes—pig—pig—pigs," murmured Freddie before he went off into another nap.

Nan helped her mother take the two little twins up to bed and then Mrs. Bobbsey sat down in the living room with Bert and Nan. They did not talk much, but listened to the storm which seemed to be getting worse all the while. It was not so much the thunder and lightning which made it a bad storm, as it was the power of the wind. Now and then, off in the forest, would sound a crash which told of some half-rotten tree falling before the gale.

At last Bert said in a low voice:

"He is very late."

"I wonder if he is coming home?" ventured Nan.

Both twins were speaking of their father, though they did not mention his name. But Mrs. Bobbsey knew whom they meant. She said:

"No, I don't believe he will get back to-night. He has probably gone so far up the lake in the motorboat, looking for Jake Doxey, that he can't get back."

"Not in all this storm," said Nan, with a little shiver as a blast of wind shook the log bungalow.

"Oh, this storm isn't much," said Bert, more because he wanted to believe that than because it was true. For it was a bad storm. "Dad knows how to run a boat," he went on. "But what makes you think he won't come back to-night, Mother?"

"Because it is getting so late and he would not want to run the boat on the lake in the storm. Then, too, he may have gotten to a place where he heard more news of Jake Doxey and he may have to keep on farther up the lake in the morning. He would lose time coming home."

"Yes, I believe he would," admitted Bert. "I guess he's at some camp. He'll be all right there."

"I wish he would telephone and let us know where he is," sighed Nan, looking toward the windows against which the rain was madly dashing.

"There aren't many telephones in this part of the woods," said Mrs. Bobbsey. "Very likely your father is in a camp that has no telephone, so he can't let us know where he is. But I'm sure he is all right."

"I hope so," murmured Nan.

"If he doesn't come by morning I'll start out and look for him," Bert declared.

"Oh, you won't need do that!" Mrs. Bobbsey exclaimed. "He will come home or send us word. And now you two had better go to bed."

"Aren't you coming too, Mother?" Nan wanted to know.

"Yes, I'll go in a little while."

Mrs. Bobbsey was really worried about her husband, but she did not want the children to know it. She pretended to be sure that he would come home in the morning. But as the wind blew harder than ever and the rain dashed down, she feared that he was in some sort of trouble with the motorboat in which he had started to look for the missing Jake Doxey.

Mrs. Bobbsey remained up a little while

after Nan and Bert had gone to bed. She listened for every sound, hoping to hear her husband's steps. But the night wore on and he did not come. At last, weary and anxious she, too, went to bed.

It was hardly daylight when Mrs. Bobbsey awakened. She had slept a little but not well, for she was, even in her slumber, more or less listening for the return of her husband.

"I' ll make a cup of coffee," said Mrs. Bobbsey to herself. "It will do me good. Then I'll go and ask Mr. Truston what is the best thing to do."

Though the campers had breakfast, as well as their other meals, in the big log dining room, those who wished could cook for themselves simple dishes on a small stove that was set up in each bungalow. Mrs. Bobbsey lighted the wood and put on some water to boil as she got out the can of coffee. The storm was over, and the sun was coming up, but the wind was still blowing hard.

There was a noise behind her and Mrs. Bobbsey started as she put some ground coffee into the pot.

"Who is that?" she asked.

"Oh, Mother, are you up?" asked Bert.

"Of course I'm up," she replied. "I'm making some coffee. But what are you doing up so early?" Bert was dressed, but Mrs. Bobbsey had only paused to put on a bath robe.

"I'm going out to look for Dad," said Bert firmly. "Maybe he lost his way in the woods or maybe he got stuck in the boat and he needs help."

"Your father is hardly likely to get lost," Mrs. Bobbsey said. "But he may have had trouble running the boat. It isn't a very good one."

"The ignition goes on the blink lots of times in those boats, especially in a storm," Bert said. "Or maybe he ran out of gas. I guess that's what happened. But I'm going to look for Dad."

"All right," agreed Mrs. Bobbsey, after a moment of thought. "It may be just as well. But you must have some breakfast first."

Bert did not want to wait for breakfast, but his mother made him do so. She had some food in the bungalow, having four ever-hungry children, though most meals were eaten in the big log dining hall.

Bert ate hurriedly and got ready to start out. As he was leaving the bungalow he and his mother saw Mr. Truston coming up the path.

"Maybe he has some news for us." said Mrs. Bobbsey.

But Mr. Truston had no good news.

"Did Mr. Bobbsey get back last night?" he asked.

"No, he didn't," said his wife. "And I'm very much worried about him. It was a terrible storm, wasn't it?"

"Pretty bad," answered the camp master. "A lot of boats got wrecked I hear."

"Boats wrecked?" cried Bert. "Why, my father is out in a motorboat! He went up the lake to find Jake Doxey."

"I know he did," said Mr. Truston. "I saw him go, but I thought he might have come in after midnight. I don't think, not for a minute, that his boat was wrecked," he added quickly, seeing that he had given Mrs. Bobbsey cause for more worry. "It's only some small craft that went on the rocks in the gale. I'm sure Mr. Bobbsey will be all right."

"I'm going to look for him!" declared Bert

bravely. "He may be stuck in some place where he can't get word out. I'm going to look for him."

"I think that's a good idea," said Mr. Truston. "But you can't go alone, can you?"

"I'll take Ned Floyd with me," was the answer.

"Just you two boys?" asked Mrs. Bobbsey anxiously.

"I'll go with them," kindly offered Mr. Truston. "We'll get up a searching party."

"I'll find my father," declared Bert as, a little later, he started off on the trail with the others.

Mrs. Bobbsey wondered what had happened to her husband.

CHAPTER XVIII

THE WILD GIRL

Bert Bobbsey had not been very long on the trail after his missing father when Flossie and Freddie, awakened earlier than usual, came out to Mrs. Bobbsey, who was clearing away the remains of the early breakfast.

"Where's Daddy?" asked Flossie, rubbing her eyes. She was not yet quite awake.

"I want to tell him about our pigs," went on Freddie. "Maybe he'll let us have one for a pet."

"And I want to tell him about how we got lost on Forest Island. Where is he?" demanded Flossie again.

"Your father hasn't come home yet," Mrs. Bobbsey answered. "He is still looking for Jake Doxey."

For a moment it seemed as if the small

Bobbsey twins were going to feel very bad about their missing father. They might even cry, Mrs. Bobbsey feared. But just when it seemed likely that the tears of Flossie, at least, might splash down on the floor, in came Mrs. Truston.

At first Mrs. Bobbsey hoped the camp master's wife would have some news about Mr. Bobbsey. But this was not so. Besides, Bert and the other searchers could hardly have had time to find him so soon. With a quick glance at Mrs. Bobbsey the camp master's wife asked:

"Are you going in the carnival?"

"What carnival?" asked the children's mother.

"Haven't you heard about it?" went on Mrs. Truston. "Oh, we have wonderful times at our water carnival! I must tell you about it. I am sure you children will want to be in it."

"Oh, tell us about it!" begged Flossie and Freddie. It was a good thing they had something new to think about or they might have cried.

"Is it a carnival on the lake and do they decorate the boats?" asked Nan, who had come down just before Flossie and Freddie, in time to bid Bert good-bye.

"Yes, all the campers decorate their boats and row around the cove," said Mrs. Truston. "There are prizes for the best decorated boat and we have lots of fun. There is also a prize for the boat with the best singers in it."

"Singers?" asked Mrs. Bobbsey. "What is that?"

"Each boatload of carnival folks is supposed to sing as they go past the stand of the judges," explained Mrs. Truston. "Those that sing best get a prize."

"I can sing," declared Flossie. "Do you want to hear me? I know a song about a pussycat and a frog."

"You may sing a little later, Flossie," her mother promised.

"Well, I can't sing now 'cause I got to have music," said the little girl. "Nan has to play for me."

"I can sing, too!" exclaimed Freddie.

"You can't sing as loud as I can," snapped Flossie. "I can sing terribly loud."

"So can I!" came from Freddie.

"Oh, you cannot!"

"Well, I can squirt my fire engine and that's more than you can do, Flossie Bobbsey!"

"Children! Children!" gently chided Mrs. Bobbsey. "Listen to Mrs. Truston tell more about the carnival. When is it to be?"

"In a few days now," was the answer. "Besides prizes for the best decorated boats and for the singers, there are prizes for the prettiest and the queerest masquerade costume worn by a boy or a girl."

"You mean like Hallowe'en?" asked Freddie.

"Yes, like Hallowe'en, only you don't have to put on a false face," the camp master's wife said. "I hope you Bobbseys will go in and try for a prize."

"Sure we will!" said Freddie.

"I'll take my doll in," promised Flossie.

"And I'll take my engine," Freddie added. "If a boat gets on fire I'll put it out."

"Well, we might need your engine at that," said Mrs. Truston, with a laugh. "Sometimes the Chinese lanterns they use to decorate the boats catch fire. But no one ever got burned."

She went on to tell more about the carnival and Flossie and Freddie were now so interested that they forgot all about their father having been out in the storm all night.

"I thought it would take their minds off worrying about their father if they had something new to think about," said the camp master's wife to Mrs. Bobbsey when Flossie and Freddie had gone outside to talk about the coming lake carnival. "They did worry, didn't they?"

"A little," Mrs. Bobbsey had to say. "I'm worried myself. Bert has gone off to look for his father."

"Yes, I know. Mr. Truston told me," said the other woman. "Oh, I'm sure he will be all right. Motorboats often get out of order and he may have had to walk back along a trail. Don't worry. I'm sure everything will be all right. And I do hope you will be in the carnival."

"Oh, yes, we'll do as the other campers do," promised Mrs. Bobbsey.

A little later she and Nan went to the dining cabin for breakfast, taking the smaller twins with them. Everybody was talking either about the storm, the coming carnival, or about Mr. Bobbsey not having been home all night.

While some of the men and women in the camp called to talk to Mrs. Bobbsey and tell her not to worry about her missing husband, Nan and Mary walked to a hill where they could have a good view of the upper part of the lake.

"We may see my father coming along in his motorboat," Nan said.

Meanwhile Flossie and Freddie had made up their minds what part they would take in the water carnival. They talked it over between themselves as they left the dining cabin and decided that to decorate a big rowboat was more than they could do.

"But we can be like Hallowe'en," decided Flossie.

"Sure, we can," agreed Freddie. "And we don't have to get any false faces. Now, Flossie," he went on, "how would you like to be a wild girl of the woods?"

"Oh, I wouldn't want to be a wild girl and live all alone in the woods," Flossie answered. "I rather be a tame girl and live in a bungalow."

"But this is only a make-believe wild girl for a little while," explained Freddie. "I can dress you up so you will look like a wild girl and you can holler and growl and make believe you are like an animal."

"I'd like to do that," Flossie said.

"And you'd be all dressed up in a piece of skin and vines and things like that," went on Freddie.

"Oh, can't I wear my own clothes?" Flossie asked.

"Course not!" exclaimed Freddie. "Who ever saw a wild girl of the woods wearing a tame girl's clothes? You have to take off most of your clothes and wear grapevines and animal skin."

"Oh! All right," agreed Flossie, after a while. "But where you going to get an animal skin?"

"There's one in the garage where we keep our car," Freddie replied. "I guess nobody will care if we take it. You'll look fine as a wild girl of the woods, Flossie."

"Yes, I'll look swell," she said. "Go ahead and dress me up. Maybe I'll get a prize."

"Maybe," agreed Freddie. "But half the prize will be mine for dressing you up."

Flossie admitted that this was fair, and they

went to the log garage not far from the bungalow. As Freddie had said, there were some
old fur auto robes hanging on the log walls.
The camp had once been the home of lumbermen and these fur robes were used in the days
when they traveled about in sleds.

"First I have to half undress you," said
Freddie to his sister. "A wild girl of the woods
has to have bare legs and bare arms."

"And must I be like a bear and growl?"
Flossie asked.

"It would be better," Freddie agreed. So it
was planned.

Flossie took off everything except her little
drawers and waist and then Freddie draped
around her a piece of an old wolf robe. He
tied it about her waist with cords.

"Now I must put some vines around you,"
he said, pulling some strands from a wild
grape that grew in the woods. "I have to wind
these vines all around you, same as a real wild
girl of the woods would do, Flossie."

"All right. Go ahead. I'll be terribly wild."

"Then I have to get some walnut juice or
some mud or something and make your face
and arms and legs dark," went on Freddie.

"Wild girls aren't as nice and white as you are."

"You're not going to rub mud on me!" exclaimed Flossie. "I don't want that."

"Then I'll stain you with walnut juice," decided Freddie. "Now you sit down and I'll twine a lot of these vines around you. We'll practice a bit and I guess you'll get a prize at the carnival."

"I hope so," said Flossie. Already she was a little tired of being wrapped in the heavy fur robe.

When Freddie did anything he put his best efforts on it. And now, when he was making Flossie a "wild girl of the woods," he decided he must use plenty of grapevine strands to bind her with. She was to pretend to be a captive wild girl.

"There, now you stay on this stump until I come back with some walnut juice to stain you brown like a Gypsy," Freddie told his sister.

"All right," she answered.

As a matter of fact, she would have had hard work to get up off the stump to walk away, for Freddie had so twined the strands of grapevine about her arms and legs and about the old stump that Flossie was like a prisoner, though at first she did not know it.

Freddie was gone some time off in the woods looking for walnuts to use the juice of the shells to color his sister brown, and Flossie grew tired of waiting.

"Freddie! Freddie!" she called. "Where are you? I'm not going to play any more. I'm going home."

Flossie struggled to get loose from the binding vine, but she could not. Freddie had made it too tight. This way and that the little girl bent and twisted, but she could not get loose. Then she began to get a little frightened and she cried and called:

"Freddie! Freddie! Come and let me loose. I don't want to be a wild girl any more."

But Freddie did not come.

CHAPTER XIX

THE BROKEN BOAT

WELL it was for poor Flossie that about this time her mother thought of coming to see what her little girl was doing. Mrs. Bobbsey had heard Flossie and Freddie say they were going off in the woods to play, not far from the bungalow, and she had heard them talking about the coming carnival.

After a while Mrs. Bobbsey began to feel less worried about her missing husband. She thought he was just staying away until he could find Jake Doxey. And with Bert and the others seeking for Mr. Bobbsey, his wife felt that if anything had happened to him his friends in camp would find and bring him home safe.

"But it's time Flossie and Freddie came back from the woods," said Mrs. Bobbsey to Nan, who, with Mary Floyd, had returned from their watch-hill, not having seen any sign of the missing father.

"Oh, I guess they're all right," Nan said rather wearily, for she was tired and worried about her father.

"I'll go and look," decided Mrs. Bobbsey, and having learned from some children in camp which way Flossie and Freddie had taken she was soon on their trail.

It was well for poor Flossie, as has been said, that her mother came when she did. Freddie had so tied and tangled his little sister in the piece of fur and the strong vine of the wild grape that Flossie could not get loose from the stump. She had been sitting on it, but her twists and wriggles had made her fall off and now she was half on the ground and half on the stump, and in a very sad state, indeed.

"Freddie! Freddie!" Flossie cried. "You come and let me loose! I don't want to be a wild girl any more."

Then, after many calls, when Freddie did not come back from his search for walnuts to stain his sister brown, Flossie cried:

"Mother! Mother!"

Luckily, just then her mother was hurrying along the path. She heard the little girl call and answered:

"What is it, my dear?"

"Oh, Mother," sobbed Flossie, "come and get me loose! I'm all tangled up!"

"You poor child! I should think you were," said Mrs. Bobbsey when she saw the state poor Flossie was in. "What in the world has happened?"

"Oh, Freddie started to make me a wild girl," Flossie sobbed. "He said I had to be like a wolf and with vines around me and he tied me up, but it's so tight I don't like it."

"I shouldn't think you would," her mother said. "Poor Flossie! Where is Freddie?" she asked, as she loosed the vines.

"He has gone to get nuts to make me brown like a Gypsy," was the answer. "'Cause wild girls can't have a white skin. But I don't want to be wild any more."

"No, indeed! I should say not!" exclaimed Mrs. Bobbsey, taking poor, sobbing Flossie up on her lap as she sat down on the stump. "But don't cry. You're all right now."

By the time Flossie was feeling better, along

came Freddie. His face and hands were stained a bright purple, and at the sight of him his mother cried:

"What in the world have you been doing?"

"Oh," answered Freddie easily, "I couldn't find any nuts to color Flossie brown, but I found some of these purple berries and they're a nice color for a wild girl."

Mrs. Bobbsey saw that he had in his hands several bunches of poke berries which stain a lovely purple color that is hard to get off one's hands and face. Then Freddie saw that Flossie was free of the wolf skin and the vines he had put on her.

"Hey!" he cried. "Don't do that! How can she be a wild girl of the woods if she isn't tied up?"

"I'm not going to be a wild girl," Flossie said.

"Oh, aren't you?" asked the little fellow in disappointed tones. "And aren't you going to let me color you purple?"

"No, I'm not!" declared Flossie decidedly.

"You have color enough on for two wild children," said Mrs. Bobbsey, trying not to laugh. "And you mustn't make a wild girl of

Flossie, either. Oh, but you're a sight!" she murmured.

"Do I look wild?" asked Freddie eagerly.

"Very wild," said his mother. "Too much so. Now wash off that stain from your hands and face."

"It won't come off," said Freddie. "When I first got some on after I picked the berries I tried to wash it off, but it wouldn't come. Then I got a lot more on and I don't care. 'Cause if Flossie won't be a wild girl, then I'll be a wild boy in the carnival."

"We'll see about that," his mother answered, as she began putting Flossie's dress back on the little girl. "Now throw those berries away and wash yourself in the brook there. You're terrible, Freddie!"

" 'Twon't do any good to wash, Mother," he said. "This color won't come off."

"I hope some of it will," Mrs. Bobbsey answered. "I'm glad I got here in time to keep you from making Flossie look like a bottle of purple ink."

"It's a good color for a wild girl," Freddie said simply, and his mother sighed and was glad it was no worse.

Freddie was right. Not much of the purple stain came off his hands and face. But his mother hoped warm water and soap might clean him up a bit when they got to the bungalow. Flossie was none the worse from having been tangled in the vines.

"If you want to take part in the carnival," said Mrs. Bobbsey, "you must pick out some other masquerade costume than that of wild children."

"All right," said Freddie after a little thought as the three walked through the woods toward camp. "I'll be a fireman."

"I can be a Red Cross nurse with my doll," said Flossie.

"That will be nice," said Mrs. Bobbsey.

Meanwhile, Bert and the others were walking through the woods up along the shore of the lake, searching for Mr. Bobbsey. They had started off along the shore nearest the bungalow camp and there was a good road close to the water, leading up over a mountain trail to the far end of Spruce Lake.

Walking along as close as they could to the water, Bert and the others in the searching party stopped now and then and called Mr.

Bobbsey's name. It seemed a bit queer to Bert and Ned that a big man, like Mr. Bobbsey, could be lost in the woods. But so it was.

"Almost anything might happen in a storm such as we had," said Mr. Truston.

"Do you think anything happened to my father?" asked Bert.

"Oh, I think he's lost, or maybe he had to land on the other side of the lake in his boat," was the answer. "But I'm sure he is all right and that we'll find him soon."

"I hope so," murmured Bert.

They walked on for several miles, and at last Ned, who had walked on a little ahead, came to a cove, or little bay, of the lake.

"Look!" he cried, pointing to a large tree that leaned out over the water.

"What is it?" asked Bert, hurrying to catch up to his chum.

"It's a boat," answered Ned. "Maybe it's the one your father went out in yesterday to look for Jake Doxey."

They were soon at the boat which was tied to the tree at the edge of the water. The boat was broken, or rather, the motor in it was broken and it could not run.

"Yes," said Mr. Truston as he looked the boat over, "that's the one your father set out in, my boy."

"But where is my father?" asked Bert, looking from the broken boat around the woods behind him and over the lake.

"I don't know where he is," the camp master said. "But we'll find him. I think he left the broken boat here and started to walk back to camp and got lost. But we'll find him!"

CHAPTER XX

NIGHT ON THE MOUNTAIN

When Bert Bobbsey first saw the broken motorboat tied to a tree at the edge of the lake and knew that it was the craft in which his father had been voyaging during the storm, the boy felt worried. But when Mr. Truston said he felt sure Mr. Bobbsey was all right and would soon be found, Bert took courage.

"Let's yell and maybe he'll hear us," suggested Ned.

"Oh, I don't believe Mr. Bobbsey is around here," said the camp master. "He saw that he couldn't get this boat going, so he started on foot back to our camp."

"Why didn't he get there, then?" asked Bert.

"Very likely he took the wrong road," suggested Mr. Truston. "That could easily happen."

"Well, then," suggested Ned, "he may have gone in a circle and wandered back here. I think it would be good to yell."

"It can't do any harm," the camp master agreed.

"All right, then let's yell all together," proposed Bert.

So they set up a great shout, calling Mr. Bobbsey's name several times. But all the answers they received were echoes and they stopped, for they saw it was doing no good.

"What shall we do next?" asked Bert, willing to leave it to Mr. Truston to make plans, for he was in charge of the searching party.

"Well," said the camp master, after thinking about it, "I don't believe Mr. Bobbsey started back by water, for we have kept pretty close to the lake shore in coming here and we didn't see anything of him. Besides, if he had started home in another boat, he would have been there by this time.

"What I think he did was to start back through the woods, and either he got lost or else he heard from some one about a new place to look for that Doxey chap and he has gone there. That's why he hasn't come back."

"But wouldn't you think he'd send word?" asked Bert, who knew that when his father was going to be later than usual in coming home from the office he always telephoned.

"There aren't any telephones in the woods outside of our camp and a few lumbermen's houses," said Mr. Truston. "Mr. Bobbsey could not find a telephone or he would have let you know. So I am sure he is in the woods. We ought to be able to find him."

"Let's go and look," suggested Bert eagerly. "Where does this trail go?" he asked, pointing to one that led up over the mountain from the place where they had found the broken boat.

"That goes to our camp, but by a round-about way," said Mr. Truston. "It is possible your father took that."

"Then I'm going to take the mountain trail and find him," Bert said. "I'll tell him how anxious Mother is and for him to hurry home. I'll find him."

"Yes, that will be a good plan," said the camp master. "The mountain trail is easy to follow, so you shouldn't get lost, Bert. And the rest of us will go back along the lake, but by a different path which Mr. Bobbsey may have taken. Between us we ought to find him pretty soon."

"I hope so," murmured Bert.

"Well, then, we'll leave you to go by the mountain trail and we'll take the old logging road," suggested Mr. Truston. "You ought to get home by dark, Bert. It's a pretty long trail, but an easy one. And if you don't find your father on it, I'm sure he will be home by the time you get there."

Thus the searching party divided, Bert going off by himself to look for his father along the high mountain trail, while Mr. Truston and the others went back to the broken boat, from which they had wandered into the woods a short distance to call Mr. Bobbsey's name. From the place where the boat was tied they would take the old logging trail back to camp.

"Maybe I'd better go with Bert," suggested Ned, seeing his chum start off alone.

"Oh, I'll be all right. I'm not afraid," said Bert. "Besides, your mother told you to stay with Mr. Truston, Ned."

"That's right, she did. But I don't like to see you go off all by yourself."

"There's no danger and the trail is very plain," said the camp master. "We'll see you later, Bert, and either you will find your father or we shall."

So they parted, but Bert was to have rather a queer adventure before he saw his friends or his father again.

However, at first he had no worries as he started off on the mountain trail. His only anxiety was about his father. Still, he felt sure that Mr. Bobbsey, who had been camping many times in wild and lonely places, could look after himself. And the fact that he had tied his broken motorboat to a tree made it certain that there had been no accident on the lake.

The sun was shining brightly for it was shortly after noon, and the party had eaten the lunch they had brought with them before Bert left to go off by himself. It was pleasant on the mountain, and had it not been that Mr. Bobbsey was lost Bert would have thought it great fun to be thus searching.

"But I'll soon find him," Bert said to himself.

Though the mountain trail was plain, having been in use many years, it was rather hard going at first, for it was all uphill. But Bert was a sturdy lad and hiked along, now and then stopping to pick some berries, now pausing to watch a squirrel or a bird flitting through the trees, and again making a halt to raise his voice in a shout, calling his father's name.

Mr. Bobbsey did not answer, and Bert kept on. Once or twice he heard rather a loud rustling of the leaves of the bushes as he passed along the trail, and he thought the noise might be caused by some large animal.

"I'd like to see a bear," thought Bert. "Maybe it would be more fun to see a bear if I had a gun, but I don't believe a bear would chase me. Mr. Truston said there weren't any bigger wild animals than foxes around here."

Though the strange rustlings sounded more than once, Bert had no glimpse of even a fox. Then a new thought came to him.

"Maybe it's a snake!" he whispered.

Bert had been told that in the part of the country where he was there were only two sorts of snakes the bite of which was poisonous. These were rattlers and copperheads.

"And even rattlers and copperheads would rather run away from you than bite you," recalled Bert. "Other snakes can't do you any harm. So I guess I'm not going to be afraid, even if that noise was made by rattlers or copperheads, which I don't believe it was."

So he traveled on, stopping now and then to look closely at the bushes whenever he heard the rustling sound again. Once he found it was caused by a thrush, a large, beautiful, brown bird which loves to scratch in the dried leaves after bugs and worms.

A second time Bert heard rather a loud rustling and saw a bright-eyed little animal with stripes on its back fur peering at him from amid a mound of stones.

"Chipmunk!" exclaimed Bert, with a laugh. "Well, I'm sure I'm not going to be afraid of you!"

Nor was the little squirrel-like chipmunk afraid of Bert, for it sat perched on a rock, looking at him brightly and then, when Bert did not go away, the chipmunk began to chatter and scold.

"I guess you're asking me what I'm doing in these woods," chuckled Bert. "Well, I'm looking for my father. Did you ever get lost, chipmunk?"

The animal chattered louder than before and might be saying almost anything.

"I'm sorry, but I don't understand your talk," the boy said, with another laugh. "And I haven't time to stay and learn it now. So I'll skip along."

He went on up the trail until he came to the top of the mountain. It was, really, rather a big hill than a mountain. On the way up Bert had paused several times and shouted for his father. He got no answer.

"But I've got quite a way to go yet," Bert told himself as he started down the trail. "I guess I'll find my father on the way home."

Whistling to himself, for it was rather lonely, Bert kept along until, suddenly, he heard a much louder noise than before in the bushes at the edge of the trail.

"That's no bird or chipmunk," murmured the boy. "Maybe it's a fox."

He heard a snarl just ahead of him and it

also seemed to come from above him. He glanced up and saw, perched on a tree branch, a grayish-yellow animal, like a big cat, but with queer tufts, or tassels of hair, on its ears.

"Hello! A bobcat! A lynx!" exclaimed Bert, who had often seen these animals in the zoo. "Well, I won't hurt you if you don't hurt me," he went on. "Scoot!" he yelled suddenly, tossing a stick he carried at the bobcat.

With another snarl, showing its sharp teeth, the lynx sprang back amid the branches of the tree and was soon slinking away. It had just come out to look at Bert from curiosity.

"Well, I'm having quite a few adventures," thought the boy as he started on again. "But the best one would be to find Dad and go home with him."

However, there was no sign of Mr. Bobbsey, nor did Bert get any answer to his further shouts. So he hurried along. He now began to notice that it was not as light as it had been. Thinking a storm might be coming, Bert looked up at the sky when he came to a clearing in the woods. But there were no clouds.

"It must be getting night," thought Bert. "It's a longer way back to camp by this mountain trail than I thought. I wish I was back, and with Dad!"

He went along a little farther and came to a place where the trail divided, one branch leading to the right and one to the left.

"I wonder which way I ought to go?" mused Bert. "Mr. Truston didn't say anything about this." He paused in bewilderment. It was getting darker and darker. Bert went a little way along the left road and, fearing it was wrong, came back and took the other path. He was not sure this was right, but decided to keep on.

Then it became very dark. He could hear the chirp of crickets and katydids, and could see bats darting about amid the trees. It was night on the mountain and Bert was almost as much lost as he had ever before been in all his life.

CHAPTER XXI

A STRANGE MEETING

Mrs. Bobbsey felt rather lonely back in camp, after Bert and the searching party had started off on the trail. Her husband was gone and so was one of her boys. Of course Nan, Freddie and Flossie were with her and she tried not to worry too much.

"I must keep cheerful for the sake of the children," thought Mrs. Bobbsey. "And of course nothing really could have happened. I think Dick has just gone off a long way into the woods to find Jake Doxey. He surely is a queer man to hide himself away as he has done."

Flossie and Freddie were too excited, talking about the coming water carnival, to think much about their father, greatly as they loved him. They felt sure he would come home all right.

So the two small twins, after the incident when Flossie was partly turned into a "wild girl," began to plan for a new masquerade.

"Will you help me be a Red Cross nurse, Nan?" Flossie asked.

"Of course I will," was the answer.

"Will you help me make a red suit so I can be a fireman?" begged Freddie.

Nan said she would and she was glad to be busy helping the little twins, for it made the time pass more quickly and brought nearer the hour when, Nan felt, her father must come home.

But there was quite an anxious time after Bert and the searching party had set out. When noon came Mrs. Bobbsey did not feel much like eating lunch, but she went to the big log cabin with the three children. Many of the other campers told her how sorry they felt for her.

"I can't see where Mr. Bobbsey can be," said his wife at last. She was back in the bungalow and she was wondering whether she had not better start out herself and look for him when she heard a step on the porch.

"Dick, is that you?" she cried eagerly, feeling sure she knew that step.

"Yes," answered Mr. Bobbsey, coming in. "I'm home at last. And such a time as I've had!"

"Are you hurt?" asked his wife anxiously, noticing that his clothes were wet and muddy and that he looked very tired.

"Oh, no, I'm not hurt," he said. "But I had a hard time in the storm. The motorboat broke down and I had to leave it quite a distance up the lake. I'll have to go after it later."

Before Mr. Bobbsey could tell any more of his adventures or explain where he had been all night, in rushed Flossie and Freddie, eager to tell about what had happened on Forest Island.

"We found pigs!" shouted Freddie.

"A big pig and little pigs," added Flossie, "and Freddie made me a wild girl and I couldn't get loose!"

Then, by fits and starts, turn and turn about, the little Bobbsey twins told their adventures, which were very big and strange to them, simple as they may appear to you. Their father listened earnestly, and Mrs. Bobbsey knew the best way was to let Flossie and Freddie have their "say" out. Otherwise, when she and her husband tried to talk they would be continually interrupted.

So, finally, the two little ones had told everything they could think of and were ready to go back with Nan, who had followed them into the bungalow. She was working with them to make masquerade costumes for the carnival.

"But where were you all night, Daddy?" asked Freddie.

"I was in the woods," he answered.

"Oh!" exclaimed the little boy. This satisfied him. He knew his father could take care of himself.

"Did you sleep under a tree?" asked Flossie.

"No, I slept in a log cabin with a lumberman."

"Oh," murmured Flossie. "Well, I'm glad you're going to sleep here with us to-night."

"So am I," said Mr. Bobbsey, with a laugh.

Then he explained to his wife what had happened. He had started out from camp in the motorboat when the picnic party went to Forest Island. Tracing Jake Doxey, Mr. Bobbsey went on and on until the storm broke and then he had to come in close to shore for fear his boat would sink. In the worst of the storm the engine of the boat got out of order and would not run any more.

"So I tied the boat to a tree and came ashore," Mr. Bobbsey told his wife.

"Then did you start for home, and have you been on the trail all night?" she asked.

"I started for home," Mr. Bobbsey said; "but on my way back through the woods, and when the storm was quite bad, I met a lumberman with his wagon. He offered me a lift and we got to talking about Jake Doxey. The lumberman thought he knew where Jake was and offered to take me there, so I rode along with him.

"The storm was so bad I felt that I couldn't get back to camp, and there was no way of letting you know where I was. But I thought you would guess that I was all right. Did you worry much?"

"Yes," answered Mrs. Bobbsey, "I did, rather. Especially when you were away all night and in the morning we heard about several boats being wrecked by the storm on the lake."

"Yes, a few boats were wrecked," said Mr. Bobbsey. "But though mine wouldn't go any more and was broken down, it wasn't exactly wrecked. Well, I rode on through the woods with the lumberman and we got to his cabin. He said I could stay there over night and in the morning he would take me where I could find Jake Doxey.

"There was no way of telephoning you or I would have done so. I didn't have a very jolly night, but in the morning the lumberman and I started out to find Jake. But that man must be as slippery as an eel," chuckled Mr. Bobbsey, "for he was gone when we got to the place where he had last been. So I decided to come on back to camp, and here I am. Is everything all right here?"

"Yes, quite all right," Mrs. Bobbsey replied. "Bert and some of the men and boys have gone on a searching party after you."

"After me?" exclaimed Mr. Bobbsey in surprise. "Bert?"

"Yes," said his wife. "I thought maybe you might meet them."

"No, I didn't. But then I came along by a back road. I hope Bert gets home all right."

"So do I," said his mother. "I should think they would be coming along pretty soon now."

"Well, I'll go and get off some of my mussy clothes," said Mr. Bobbsey. "And then if Bert and his rescue party haven't come back I may have to go out after them."

As soon as Mr. Bobbsey had changed his clothes loud talking was heard down near the lake, and Nan came running up to the bungalow to say that Mr. Truston and the other searchers had returned.

"But Bert isn't with them," Nan stated.

"Bert not with them!" exclaimed Mr. Bobbsey. "Why, where is he? Why didn't he come back with them?"

Mr. Truston came up to the bungalow and explained how Bert had decided to take the mountain trail to look for his father, leaving the others to come back by the lake path, which they had done.

Then passed several anxious hours of waiting for Bert to return. But he did not appear and night settled down over Flat Rock Camp. Both Mr. and Mrs. Bobbsey were worried now.

"Where is Bert?" asked Freddie when he heard his brother had not come home.

"In the woods," Mr. Bobbsey answered.

"But I guess he is all right and will be home soon."

"Maybe a bear will eat him up," said Flossie, gloomily.

"There aren't any bears in these woods," said her mother, and that made Flossie and Freddie feel better.

Meanwhile, Bert was having troubles of his own. He had come to the place where the trail divided just as it was getting dark and did not know which road to take. At last he turned to the right and hurried along that, hoping it would soon bring him to where his father was, or back to Flat Rock Camp, or to some place where he could find shelter.

It grew darker and darker and there was no sign of Mr. Bobbsey or the camp or shelter of any kind. Bert was a brave, sturdy lad but he thought if he kept on traveling along a strange trail in the darkness he might get into trouble.

"I guess I'd better make some sort of a shelter and stay here until morning," Bert at last decided. "It isn't going to be any fun, for I'll be hungry and I won't have much of a bed. But I'll do the best I can."

By the light of the stars he traveled on until he came to a small clearing, or open place, in the woods. He dimly made out a big, overhanging rock against a side hill and thought that would be as good a shelter as he could find. There were some dried leaves on the ground beneath the rock and they made a fairly good bed. Bert broke some branches off a hemlock tree to spread over him for covers.

"Now all I want is something to eat and a drink of water and I'll be in pretty good shape," he murmured to himself. He did not remember having put them in his pockets, but he was overjoyed to find part of a sandwich and some crackers left over from the lunch he had brought from home that morning.

"This is going to taste good!" exclaimed Bert. He ate hungrily, wishing he had more. Then he felt thirsty, and in the stillness of the night he heard a trickle of water not far from his rock shelter. He soon discovered a spring at which he drank.

Then, feeling much better, though he was worried about his mother and the folks at home, Bert curled up and tried to sleep. At first he could not, for there were many strange noises in the woods all about him—noises made by wild animals, Bert was sure. But he had seen the lynx run away from him and knew no fox would come near, so he did not feel afraid. At last he fell asleep.

It was morning when he awakened, cold, damp, stiff, and hungry. But he crawled out into the sun, ran up and down a little to exercise and get warm, and then he was ready to start off again.

"It isn't much of a breakfast," said Bert with a smile as he drank at the spring. "But I'll soon be home, I hope."

He traveled on as the sun rose higher and higher and, before he knew it, he was on a new trail which took him back to Spruce Lake but at a point he had not been before.

"Well, I'm not lost, anyhow," said Bert to himself. "I can follow the lake shore and get back to our camp."

He paused for a moment to look out over the water from a little hill when he suddenly heard, below him, the put-put of a motorboat.

"Oh, maybe that's Dad!" exclaimed the boy eagerly. "Hey, Dad! Dad!" he shouted.

There was no answer, but Bert ran down the

hill toward the little cove whence came the sound. Turning around a point of trees, Bert saw a craft drifting in toward shore. The sound of the engine had now stopped.

A glance showed Bert it was not his father in the boat. It was a boy—a boy whom Bert had seen before. It was strange to meet him again on Spruce Lake.

"Hello there!" cried Bert.

"Hello!" answered the other boy, and, as he looked up while the boat drifted nearer and nearer to shore, Bert made certain that it was Frank Denton—the runaway boy who had tumbled out of the overturned junk wagon.

CHAPTER XXII

A STORMY CRUISE

"Hello!" said Bert Bobbsey again, as the drifting boat gently bumped against the bush-covered bank of Spruce Lake.

"Hello!" said Frank Denton for the second time. Then he asked: "What are you doing here?"

"We're camping," Bert answered. "Not exactly here," he went on, as he looked about the shore and did not remember to have seen it before. "But down at Flat Rock."

"What are you doing so far up here?" Frank wanted to know. "And say, you look as if you had slept in the open all night," he added, as he glanced at Bert's mussed clothes.

"I was out all night," answered the Bobbsey lad. "I slept under a rock on dried leaves. My father is lost and I was out in the woods looking for him."

"Your father lost," murmured Frank. "Did he run away?"

"No, of course he didn't!" exclaimed Bert. "But you——"

He looked sharply at Frank but did not know what else to say. He remembered that Frank had run away before, when he was found hidden in among the bundles of papers on the junk wagon. But Frank had been taken back to his home in Crescent Falls. And now——

"Yes, I've run away again," said Frank, guessing what Bert's silence meant.

"You have? What for?" Bert was much surprised.

"I'll not stand for my father licking me!" muttered the Denton boy. "I told him I'd run away again if he laid his hands on me and he did so I did."

"How did you get up here from Crescent Falls in that boat?" asked Bert. He knew Spruce Lake did not go down as far as Crescent Falls.

"I hocked rides and walked from Crescent Falls to Spruce Lake," explained Frank. "I thought maybe I could get a job in one of the camps. But my father must have followed me, for yesterday, when I was tramping along, going from one camp to the next, I saw him after me. So I jumped into this motorboat and started up the lake."

"Whose boat is it?" asked Bert.

"I don't know. I just borrowed it at a camp where nobody was looking. I meant to take it back, but I can't get it running again."

"Did you have it running at first?" Bert wanted to know.

"Sure. It ran fine after I started it when my father almost caught me and I gave him the slip. But just before you hollered it stopped and I couldn't get it started. I didn't know who you were at first."

"And I didn't know you," Bert said, as he stepped into the boat now close to the bank.

"What are you going to do?" asked Frank, as he looked from Bert to the now quiet motor and then back at the Bobbsey lad.

"I'm going to find my way back to our camp if I can," Bert answered. "And I want to find my father, too. I think you had better go back to your home," he added. "I don't believe your folks will like to have you running away so much."

"Then why doesn't my father stop licking me?" asked Frank in a fretful voice. "If he'll leave me alone I'll stay at home."

"Why don't you tell him that?" suggested Bert.

"Maybe I will," was the answer. "But I came a pretty good distance in this boat when I got away from my father the second time, and now it's busted. I don't know how I'm going to get back. Do you know how to run a motorboat?" he asked Bert.

"Not much," was the reply. "My father has one at his lumber dock in Lakeport, and I've been out in it lots of times and once or twice he's let me steer it. I've started the motor, too, and shut it off. But when anything got the matter with it I didn't know how to fix it. Maybe you haven't any gasoline."

"Oh, yes, there's gasoline," said Frank. "Listen and you can hear it slop around in the tank up in front when I rock the boat."

He swayed to and fro, the motorboat tilted from side to side and, above the lapping of the water against her sides, Bert could hear the swish of gasoline in the bow tank.

"Well, maybe if I start it she'll go," said

the Bobbsey lad, after looking over the machinery and finding it something like that in his father's craft. "Can you steer?"

"Sure," Frank answered. "You get the boat started and I'll steer her all right."

Bert once more carefully looked over the boat. He did as he had often seen his father or one of the men from the lumber dock do when that boat wouldn't run. Bert made sure that there were no broken wires. He knew there was gasoline in the tank.

"Well," he said at last, "if the ignition is all right and you have gas maybe the gas isn't feeding into the carburetor. The gasoline feed pipe may be stopped up."

"How do you unstop it?" asked Frank.

"You have to unscrew this jigger here," and Bert pointed to a sleeve nut coupling on the end of the copper pipe. "Sometimes dirt gets in. You have to have a wrench and you have to shut the gas off at the tank."

"I can do that," Frank said, "and I saw some tools under one of the seats. Maybe there's a wrench."

Bert found one. The gasoline was shut off

by a little faucet at the bottom of the bow tank and then Bert unscrewed the copper pipe coupling to the carburetor. Some gasoline dropped out and with it some particles of dirt.

"There, I guess that's where the trouble was," he said. "The line was stopped."

"Well, if it's unstopped now," said Frank, "screw the pipe back and we'll see if she'll start."

In a little while the gasoline was again turned on. Bert threw on the ignition switch and Frank turned over the flywheel, which had to be done on this kind of an engine, there being no self-starter.

The motor coughed and spluttered a little, fired once or twice, stopped again; and at last started. The boat began to move out from the bank.

"Hurray!" cried Frank. "Here we go again!"

"It's great!" shouted Bert, so delighted with having got the craft started that, for a moment, he forgot about his missing father and about being lost himself.

"Now we'll travel!" went on Frank. "Which way you want to go?" he asked his new friend.

"To Flat Rock Camp," Bert answered. "But I'm awfully hungry. I wonder if we can get anything to eat on the way there."

"I have some grub left," stated Frank. "I brought some with me when I ran away. It's under that seat," and he pointed to one that raised up on a hinge.

Bert found some sandwiches and a piece of cake and these he ate hungrily, Frank saying he had had some a while ago, that being his breakfast.

The boys had been so taken up with getting the boat to run again that they had not noticed another storm coming up and as they were cruising slowly along, heading as best they knew for Flat Rock Camp, they were startled by a clap of thunder.

Almost at the same moment the motor gave a sort of cough and sneeze and stopped. Then the wind began to blow, making the lake rough, and the boys found themselves heading toward a rocky shore in a boat which was drifting before the wind.

The storm rapidly grew worse, rain falling and lightning hissing over the waves of the lake. Time and again Frank spun the flywheel, trying desperately to start the motor, but it was of no avail.

"We're going on the rocks!" cried Bert, as they neared the shore and he recognized the danger.

"Maybe I can steer into that cove," said Frank, pointing to one where it would be safer to make a landing. "Gosh, what a storm this is!"

CHAPTER XXIII

THE RAGGED MAN

It can well be imagined when night came and Bert was not to be found that both his father and mother were much worried.

"I don't see where poor Bert can be," Mrs. Bobbsey said, over and over again, when darkness had fallen and nothing had been heard from the missing boy. All that Mr. Truston, Ned, and the others could say was that Bert had started off on the trail over the mountain to find his lost father. "Oh, where can Bert be?" sighed Mrs. Bobbsey over and over again.

"He must be out in the woods, but he is perfectly safe," said Mr. Bobbsey. "I was out in those same woods and there is nothing to harm any one."

"Aren't there bears?" asked Flossie.

"No, indeed, my little fairy!"

"And no tigers?" asked Freddie.

"Of course not, my little fireman."

"Then I guess Bert is all right and he'll come home to breakfast," Flossie went on. "And, Mother," she asked, "will you please look at the Red Cross suit Nan made for me to see if it's all right for the carnival?"

"And I wish you'd sew some more brass buttons on my fireman uniform," begged Freddie. "I want a lot of brass buttons."

"Not now, my dears," said Mrs. Bobbsey, nervously walking up and down the floor. "Some other time—to-morrow."

The truth was she was so worried about Bert that she could not take any interest in the smaller twins' preparations for the coming water carnival. Mr. Bobbsey was also anxious, but not as much so as was his wife.

Nan, too, felt anxious about her missing brother and when she was talking about him to Mary, after a late supper, Nan said:

"I'd like to go right out and hunt for Bert."

"Let you and me go with Ned, to-morrow," proposed the little Floyd girl, and Nan agreed.

Meanwhile, Mr. Bobbsey had told his wife that if Bert did not return by morning they would organize all the campers into a searching party and go out along the mountain trail.

"Then we'll be sure to find Bert," he said. "But I'm sure he has had to do just what I did last night—sleep in the woods. He may have found a lumberman's log cabin and be safe and snug in it."

"Let us hope so," said his wife. She would have been glad if a searching party had started out that night, but many of the men of Flat Rock Camp were away then and it was thought best to wait until morning.

All the other campers told Mrs. Bobbsey there was no danger to Bert even if he should have to sleep in the woods all night, as he really did.

She and her husband went to bed at last, after Nan had been allowed to remain up later than usual. But neither Mr. nor Mrs. Bobbsey slept well. They were ready to get up at the slightest noise, hoping and thinking that Bert was coming in.

But the night passed without a sign of the boy and when morning came his mother insisted that a rescue party start off as soon as breakfast could be served and eaten. To this

Mr. Bobbsey agreed and he and the camp master prepared to head the seekers.

Meanwhile, Bert had passed a safe, if not very happy, night under the ledge of rock and when morning came—the same morning on which his father and the others were getting ready to look for him—Bert got back to the lake and went in the boat with Frank Denton.

"This sure is a fierce storm!" exclaimed Bert, as he tried to guide the motorboat away from the rocks and toward the safer landing on the bush-lined shore.

"It came up all of a sudden," added Frank. "The next time I run away I won't take a boat I don't know anything about."

"You'd better not run away any more," advised Bert. "I think you're making a mistake."

"Well, maybe I am," Frank said. "I'll go back and see how my father treats me."

"We've got to get ashore first, before you can go back to Crescent Falls," observed Bert. "And it isn't going to be easy."

"If we could only get this engine started again we could work the boat better," Frank said.

But now the craft was pitching and tossing on the wild waves of the lake which were being whipped into foam by the strong wind, and it was as much as the boys could do to hold on and try to steer to the safest place on the shore. A drifting boat is much harder to steer than one which goes forward by oars or the propeller.

"If she goes on the rocks she'll break all up," observed Bert a little later, noting how close they were to the sharp stones.

"And then I'll be in a pickle," muttered Frank. "It will be my fault for jumping in this boat to run away from my father. I'll get rats for this!"

"I'll have my father do what he can for you," proposed Bert. "Do you know whose boat this is?"

"No. But I can tell you what camp I took it from. It's from the one below where you are."

"I think they call that Hemlock Camp," stated Bert. "Hold fast!" he called, as there came a sudden fierce gust of wind.

But if the blast alarmed the boys, it also did them good service, for it turned the head of the boat about, headed it straight for the little cove where the shore was of sand and dirt instead of stones and so made possible a safe landing.

A few minutes after this the bow of the motor craft bumped into the shore and Bert and his new chum leaped out, holding the mooring rope of the boat. They scrambled up the shore and made the line fast to a tree. And now the rain stopped and the weather began to clear. It had been only a sudden squall.

"Well, we're safe on shore, anyhow," observed Bert, as he shook some of the rain water out of his hair and eyes. "But where are we, anyhow?"

"I don't know," Frank said. "I'm a stranger up around this part of the lake. I know one thing, though."

"What's that?" asked Bert.

"I'm not going to try to run a motorboat again until I know more about 'em. I'll walk the rest of the way back home or go in a rowboat."

"I guess it would be safer," admitted Bert. "But I wish I knew which way to go home."

"Let's walk up over the hill and maybe we can find a farmhouse," suggested Frank. "I'm still hungry."

They made sure the disabled boat was firmly tied and then started up the bank. They followed a path which ascended for a short distance and then dipped again until they came to a small clearing on the edge of the quiet little cove. There, sitting with his back against a tree and near him a string of fish, was a ragged, sleeping man, with a rough, straggly black beard. He seemed to be a tramp.

"Look!" whispered Bert to his chum.

"I don't like his looks," remarked Frank. "A touch customer, if you ask me. Come on, let's beat it!"

Bert was going to say this was good advice, but a second thought made him wonder if it would not be wise to awaken the man and ask him the best way to get back to Flat Rock Camp. While the boys hesitated and were almost ready to go away and let the man sleep, he suddenly awakened.

CHAPTER XXIV

DOWN THE LAKE

"Hello, there!" called the ragged man in greeting.

The boys did not answer.

"Hello," he said again, and he smiled. His voice was friendly and Bert began to feel less afraid. He was about to put a question to the stranger, about where they might be and about getting back to camp, when the man moved, put his string of fish to one side, got to his feet, smiled again and said:

"I guess I must have been asleep."

"You were," stated Frank.

"I hope we didn't wake you up," ventured Bert.

"Well, you did. There's no getting away from that," said the ragged man. "But there's no harm done. It was time I woke up if I'm going to cook these fish. Who are you lads, anyhow?"

Bert was pondering whether to let Frank answer first, for he was not sure how much of his story the runaway boy wanted to tell, when the ragged man caught sight of the motorboat. It seemed to surprise him. He walked down to the shore quickly, looked the boat over, and then turned back toward the boys.

"Where'd you steal that boat?" he asked, and his voice was no longer pleasant.

"I didn't steal it," said Bert.

"That boat belongs to Hemlock Camp. I know it!" exclaimed the man. "It's just below Flat Rock Camp. There aren't many boats on this lake I don't know, and I say that one is from Hemlock Camp and you lads stole it."

"The boat is from Hemlock Camp all right," said Frank. "But I didn't steal it. I just borrowed it to get away from my father."

"You did?" cried the "tramp," as the boys called the ragged man. "What did you want to get away from your father for?"

"He was chasing me."

"Why?"

"To give me a licking."

For a moment the man looked from Frank to

Bert and then back to Frank. Then he smiled through his black whiskers and said:

"There must be some story back of this. You'd better tell me all about it and I'll know better what to do. Are you borrowing motor-boats to get away from your father, too?" he asked Bert.

"Oh, no, sir! I'm lost and I just found Frank."

"Maybe you're both lost!" chuckled the tramp. "Well, let's hear your story," and he nodded at Frank.

This was soon told, from the time when the Bobbseys first met Frank as he fell out of the junk wagon until Bert came upon him a little while before.

"So your name is Bobbsey, is it?" asked the man, turning to Bert. "I know a Mr. Richard Bobbsey. He's a big lumber dealer of Lakeport. Any relation to him?"

"He's my father," answered Bert, glad that this man was turning out to be a friend.

"Your father? Well, well! This is quite a surprise! When you get back home tell your father you met Jake Doxey."

"*Jake Doxey!*" cried Bert, and there was so

much surprise in his voice that the man looked queerly at him.

"Why, yes," he said, slowly. "I'm Jake Doxey."

"Oh, my father has been looking all over for you!" cried Bert excitedly. "We came to Flat Rock Camp to look for you, but they said you were out in the woods and my father couldn't find you. He went out to look for you two days ago and he didn't come back to our bungalow all night so I went out to look for him. I got lost and I was out in the woods all night myself and I was trying to get home when I met Frank in this boat."

"Well, you had some adventures," chuckled Mr. Doxey. "But why is your father looking for me?"

"He wants to buy some land from you," reported Bert. "It's land around here, at Spruce Lake. He wants it for lumber. You were going to sell it to him a while ago."

"Oh, so that's what the deal is, eh?" and Mr. Doxey laughed again. "I didn't think he would ever want my timberland. Well, I'm willing to sell if I get my price. I've been out in the woods the last month all by myself, traveling from place to place."

"Were you lost?" asked Bert, for he and the other twins had come to believe this about Jake Doxey.

"Oh, no, I wasn't lost!" chuckled the ragged man. "But I got sort of sick and run down and the doctor said it would be good for my health to put on my oldest, raggedest clothes and rough it in the woods like a tramp. So that's what I've been doing. I've been sleeping out, catching fish when I got hungry and cooking them, and, now and then, stopping in at some lumberman's shack for a meal. I feel fine now and I'm ready to go back to my home. I haven't had a letter or talked on the telephone since I started out, and hardly any one knew where I was."

"That's what made it so hard for my father to find you, I guess," said Bert. "But he'll be glad to see you now, for ᵢₙ ⁻ⁿᵗs to buy that land. I mean he will if he's got back home and isn't lost any more," and Bert felt a little worried, for he did not then know that his father was safe back in camp.

"Oh, he'll be all right," said Mr. Doxey. "I

know Mr. Bobbsey quite well. He's able to look after himself in the woods, even if his motorboat did break down. And, speaking of this boat you borrowed," and he smiled at Frank, "what's the matter with it?"

"Busted," answered the runaway boy.

"Busted, eh? Well, I know something about boats and maybe I can get it to running again. But first what about grub? Are you lads hungry?"

"Are we?" cried Bert and there was no mistake about it.

"Same here!" echoed Frank.

"Well then we'll have a meal, for I can eat something myself. Then I'll see if I can't get this boat to running and take you boys home. You'd better go back and make it up with your father," he told Frank.

"I will," was the reply. "I've had enough of running away."

Back in the bushes Mr. Doxey had a regular camping outfit and in less time than seemed possible to the hungry boys they were sitting at a flat stump for a table and eating fried fish and corn bread which Mr. Doxey had in a bundle. It was a good meal.

"I'm certainly glad we met you, Mr. Doxey," said Bert, as he took another helping of fish.

"So am I," mumbled Frank. "I was terribly hungry."

"And my father will be glad to see you," went on Bert.

"Well, maybe it's going to be lucky all around," Mr. Doxey said. "If I can get your borrowed boat going it won't take us long to scoot down the lake to Flat Rock."

When the meal was over and the little camp broken, Mr. Doxey proved that he was an expert on motorboats, for he soon had the one Frank had taken throbbing away and ready for the trip.

"Now then, all aboard!" called Mr. Doxey.

Frank and Bert got in and, with Mr. Doxey steering, they started down Spruce Lake to Flat Rock Camp.

Meanwhile, there were many anxious hearts in that little settlement of the woods. When many hours passed and Bert had not come back, Mr. Bobbsey began to share his wife's worry and at last he made up his mind that he must go back over the mountain trail to find his lost son.

Nan was as much worried as were her father and mother, but she tried to take care of Flossie and Freddie to help Mrs. Bobbsey. The younger twins were full of the coming carnival, and with their new friends, Jerry and Susan, who were also to take part, they were busy getting their costumes ready, trying them on several times in one morning. Nan also hoped to go in the carnival.

"But it won't be any fun without Bert," she sadly said.

"Oh, I'll soon find Bert and bring him back," said Mr. Bobbsey, who was getting ready to start off on the search.

"Take us with you!" begged Freddie. "I want to find Bert."

"No, you can't go," said their mother.

"Why not?" Freddie wanted to know. "I could take my fire engine and if the trees start to burn I could put them out."

"No," said his father, "we shall have to hurry over the mountain trail and you must stay at home."

"Will you take a gun, Daddy, when you go to look for Bert?" asked Flossie. holding her doll Goldie upside down because she was so worried about her lost brother.

"A gun! What for?" asked Mr. Bobbsey.

" 'Cause I'm sure a bear has got Bert," answered the little girl, "and you ought to shoot the bear. So you'd better take a gun."

"Bert is all right—he's just lost," Mr. Bobbsey said. "And there aren't any bears. Don't worry. I'll soon be back with him. Be good children now."

Mr. Bobbsey kissed Flossie and Freddie, nodded to his wife and Nan and started out of the bungalow. For Mr. Truston and some of the other men from the camp were waiting for him to join them in a searching party.

Nan hurried out ahead of her father. She was going to beg him to let her go with him, but she did not want the younger twins to hear what she said. Just as she got out on the porch and looked toward the lake she gave a sudden shout of surprise.

CHAPTER XXV

SAFE IN CAMP

"WHAT's the matter?" called Mr. Bobbsey, hurrying out to the porch of the bungalow, where Nan had gone just ahead of him.

"See that motorboat coming!" Nan exclaimed, pointing to it. "Isn't that Bert in it?"

"Why, of course it is!" cried Mrs. Bobbsey, following her husband out on the porch. "Oh, Bert! I'm so glad you are back safe! Where have you been?"

Bert was too far away to answer, and he could not hear what his mother asked on account of the noise the engine was making. Mr. Doxey had it fixed after a fashion, but the muffler was broken and the machinery was making much more noise than it should have made.

Then Nan caught sight of two other figures in the boat. She started to run down toward the little dock for which Mr. Doxey was heading the boat. Mr. and Mrs. Bobbsey followed.

"That other boy!" exclaimed Nan. "He's Frank Denton! The one we found in the junk wagon."

"So it is!" ejaculated Mrs. Bobbsey. "I wonder what he is doing in the boat with Bert! And who is that man who looks so like a tramp?"

But at the sight of this "tramp" the eyes of Mr. Bobbsey opened wide in surprise. He now had a good look at the three in the boat. He recognized Frank Denton, saw that Bert was safe and unharmed, but at the sight of the man steering, Mr. Bobbsey excitedly cried:

"Hurray! My search is over. I've found him!"

"Who?" asked his wife. "Do you mean Bert?"

"No, I mean that man. It's Jake Doxey, the man I've been hunting for ever since we came to camp. I want to buy the timber tract from him. Well, well! I certainly am glad to see him!"

Mr. Bobbsey hurried out on the dock, followed by his wife, Nan, and members of the searching party who now need not start out to look for Bert. For Bert was here. The voyage down the lake had been made safely. Nothing had happened except that the motor stopped once or twice, but Mr. Doxey got it to going again.

"Oh, Bert!" cried his mother. "I'm so glad you're back!"

"I'm glad to be back," answered Bert.

"Where were you last night?" asked Nan.

"I slept in the woods, under a rock. It was fun!" Bert could call it fun now, but at the time, with darkness all around him and small wild animals making queer noises, it did not seem very pleasant.

"You remember Frank Denton, don't you?" Bert asked his folks. "It's lucky I met him in this boat or I might be back in the woods yet."

"Of course I remember Frank," said Mrs. Bobbsey, with a smile, as she greeted the runaway boy. "We are glad you met him again."

By this time Mr. Doxey was out on the dock beside the boys, having made the boat fast, and he and Mr. Bobbsey were shaking hands and laughing together.

"I certainly am glad to see you," said Mr. Bobbsey. "I've been looking all over for you, Mr. Doxey."

"I'm sorry you had so much trouble, Mr. Bobbsey. When I went off by myself into the woods I had no idea anybody would want me on business about my timber tract. But I'm glad to sell it to you."

"Come up to the bungalow," suggested Mr. Bobbsey, "and we'll talk the matter over. But I want to thank Mr. Truston and all my camp friends here for getting ready to go with me in search of Bert. The party is off," he said, with a laugh.

"A good ending," added the camp master.

"Just a minute now," said Mr. Doxey to Mr. Bobbsey. "I took charge of these two lads," and he nodded at Bert and Frank, "when they were lost and in trouble with their crippled motorboat. I've got one boy safe back home, but what about you?" and he looked at Frank.

"Oh, I guess I can take this motorboat back to Hemlock Camp," said the runaway lad who seemed in much better spirits since falling in with Bert. "Then I'll manage to get back to Crescent Falls. I'll go home and not run away any more."

"Good idea," said Mr. Doxey. "A boy should be friends with his father."

There was quite a little throng about the returned ones and as the crowd broke up a stranger was seen coming down to the dock. None of the Bobbseys or their friends knew who he was, but at the sight of him Frank exclaimed:

"Here's my father now!"

For a moment he seemed afraid and as if he would like to go away again, but Mr. Denton came forward and said:

"Hello, Frank, my boy. I've been looking for you these last three days. I just now heard you were around some camp up here, and I'm glad I've found you. I want to tell you, Frank, that you were right and I was wrong. I'm sorry I punished you and I want you to forgive me and let's be friends."

"That's the way to talk!" exclaimed Mr. Doxey.

"All right, Dad," said Frank, after a moment's pause. "I'm sorry I ran away, but I didn't like to be licked."

"Don't blame you," replied his father. "Well, it won't happen again."

Father and son were soon together and after hearing the story of what had happened and thanking the Bobbseys and Mr. Doxey, the two Dentons got in the boat and went on down the lake. Mr. Denton said he would leave the boat where it belonged, at Hemlock Camp, and would hire another to take him to the end of the lake where he could get an auto bus for Crescent Falls.

"Good-bye!" called Bert to his runaway chum as the motorboat puffed away from the dock.

"Good-bye!" echoed Frank. "See you again sometime, maybe."

There was a happy reunion among the Bobbsey twins and their parents and after Bert had told all his adventures and had learned about his father having come home the day before, Flossie and Freddie had to have their turn.

"Did a bear eat you?" asked Flossie anxiously.

"No, of course I wasn't eaten by a bear!" laughed Bert. "Else how could I come home?"

"Oh, well, I thought maybe you got away," said Flossie.

"I guess you wished you had my fire engine, didn't you?" asked Freddie.

"Your fire engine! What for?" asked Bert.

"To squirt water on the wolves."

"Ha! Ha! There weren't any wolves!" chuckled Bert. "The largest wild animal I saw was a bobcat and he slunk away after showing me his teeth. Oh, I got along all right."

"It was very brave of you to start out to find me all alone," said Mr. Bobbsey, as he got ready to go up to the bungalow with Mr. Doxey.

"I'm glad I did," said Bert.

"And now," said Flossie, when the others of the camp had gone away, "you'd better get ready to be in the water carnival, Bert."

"What kind of a suit are you going to wear?" asked Freddie.

"I haven't had much time to think about a water carnival," replied Bert. "Let's hear more of it."

Thereupon the small twins began to talk fast

over the parts they were to play and Nan, who was sitting near Bert, glad in her heart that he was safe with her again, said:

"Let's go in, Bert, you and me, and trim up our rowboat."

"Sure!" he agreed. "I'll tog up like an Indian."

"And I'll be a Puritan maid," echoed Nan. "I can easily make a dress like those they used to wear."

"I won't have to wear many clothes," chuckled Bert. "I'll stain my body like an Indian and put on lots of feathers."

"We're going to have Chinese lanterns on our boat," said Flossie.

"And I'll take my fire engine to squirt water if any of the lanterns take fire!" suggested Freddie.

Now that the lost ones were safe, Mrs. Bobbsey could give some thought to the coming carnival. Mr. Bobbsey, too, after having arranged to buy Jake Doxey's land, said he would help with the celebration.

This water carnival of Flat Rock Camp was to be a great event, for it was to mark the close of the season. Camp must soon break up.

for it was autumn and even the very latest of
the private schools which many of the camp
children attended were preparing to open.
Mr. Bobbsey received word that the Lakeport
school, where his twins went, would start the
first session in another week.

"So we'll have a grand time at the carnival
and then go home," said Mr. Bobbsey.

Father, mother and both sets of twins
worked hard to do their share in making the
carnival a success. So did all the other campers
not only around Flat Rock, but at Hemlock
and other places around Spruce Lake. It was
a large affair and many fine prizes were
awarded for the best decorated boats and for
individual costumes.

At last the great day, or rather, great night
came. It was a beautiful evening, calm and
peaceful, with a round moon making the lake
a sheet of silver. The Bobbsey boat was gay
with lanterns and, true to his promise, Freddie had his fire engine on board in case anything happened. But nothing did.

Mr. Bobbsey and his wife rowed the boat
containing the children in a procession of other
boats and the scene was most beautiful. On a

floating platform in the lake, around which the boats circled, a band played lively music. There was singing in all the boats and the Bobbseys did their share.

Bert made up to look like a very real Indian, and Nan was a very sweet little Puritan maid in the bow of their boat. Freddie was fitted out to look like a fireman and everyone said Flossie was the cutest little Red Cross nurse they had ever seen.

The Bobbsey boat did not win a prize, for there were others much more gaily decorated. But Mr. and Mrs. Bobbsey had not had much time to do this work, owing to the two lost ones.

However Nan and Bert received a prize for two of the best costumed children of their class, and, to the delight of Flossie and Freddie, they, also, received a prize given for the best pair of small children. Happier twins would have been hard to find that night. The only thing Freddie was sorry over was that no fire occurred so he could use his engine.

"Oh, didn't we have a lovely time?" murmured Nan, when, late that night, their boat was docked and they went slowly up to the bungalow.

"It was great!" said Bert.

"We're coming up here again next year, aren't we? I like it here," said sleepy Flossie to her mother.

"We'll see, my dear," was the answer.

"Then maybe there'll be a forest fire I can squirt water on from my engine," Freddie murmured. "I'll put it out."

"Well, you're going to be put to bed now," chuckled his father.

And so the Bobbsey twins had pleasant dreams. Not dreams of the fun in the days to come, for this they could not guess. But soon they were to make plans for Christmas. The story is called "The Bobbsey Twins' Wonderful Secret." And wonderful it was to be, indeed. But now we leave them sleeping snugly, getting ready for the next day's adventure.

THE END